AF344754

DETECTIVE NOVELS
BY THE SAME AUTHOR

Series: An investigation by Police Commissioner Vétoldi

1 - La Grosse qui mangeait des bonbons, *in Paris and Carnac*

2 - Un Fric-Frac peu catholik, *in Auxerre*

3 - Mortel Rendez-vous, *in Paris and New york*

4 - The Wild Lover, *in Provence*

5 - Meurtre à l'Assemblée, *at tyhe National Assembly*

6 - Attentat à Belle-Île, *in Belle-Île*

7 - Le Ruban rouge, *in Paris*

8 - Meurtrière sans le savoir, *in Paris*

9 - Le Roi du poulet, *in South Brittany*

10 - Meurtres au programme, *in Belle-Île*

11 - Sur le sable, *in Belle-Île*

12 - Bus mortel, *in Paris*

13 - Duo brisé, *in Belle-Île*

14 - La Rescapée de Vannes, *in Vannes*

15 - The White Dog Killer, *in Vannes*

16 - Mère indigne, *in Vannes*

17 - Gage toxique, *in Paris*

18 - Meurtre d'une diva, *in Paris and Istanbul*

Series: The Investigations of Samantha Gosvenor, FBI Agent

1 - Fatal Delivery, *in Chicago*

The novels are on sale, in digital version
on Amazon.fr and Amazon.com
In print on www.amazon.fr - www.journaux.fr
and at the Port Maria Bookstore in Quiberon.

Current serial

petitspolarsentreamis.blogspot.com

FATAL DELIVERY

Publisher: Marie Auberger
SASU S.DEGENINVILLE
18 Rue des Lavandières
56170 QUIBERON

ISBN : 978-2-9583309-4-1

Photo credits : Shutterstock/m.mphoto
Cover and typeset: Leslie Guyon (2LI.fr)

SUSAN DEGENINVILLE

FATAL DELIVERY

SAMANTHA GOSVENOR, FBI AGENT
INVESTIGATION 1

Map of Chicago Surroundings

Map developed from the maps of the following sites: Via Michelin.fr and Rome2rio.com

1
Nick Kowalski, delivery driver at Pigeon Transport

Nick was coming to his first stop. He had in mind the 150 deliveries to be made this day. He stopped his truck, leaving the engine running. Stressed by the program, he forgot his sprained ankle. He jumped out of the truck. The pain was searing. He froze, unable to take a step. Yet, this morning, before leaving, Sarah had bandaged it tightly, very happy to have found at the drugstore, an elastic and firm bandage recommended for sprains.

He smiled despite the pain, remembering his partner's words:

"I hesitated between this band and a latex anklet. The seller convinced me that the band would be more suitable, because it would follow the variations of the volume of your ankle."

Clinging to the door of his truck, Nick chased away the pain for a minute. What would his life be without Sarah, without her faithful support?

Their meeting dated from the first year of college. They had not left each other since. Their higher education stopped there. Forced to work, they had failed their exams. At the time, they had laughed about it, they had even celebrated their failure with vodka. Seven years ago...

Nick sighed and glanced at his load. A mountain of boxes awaited their delivery.

He was late. He hobbled to the back of the vehicle and opened the doors to access the first package. He walked towards his client's house. Seeing him, two huge dogs sprang from their niche. They stretched their chain as much as they could. Despite his fright, Nick didn't back down, he could almost smell their breath and see the drool dripping from their mouths. A cold sweat ran down his forehead, he would have liked to do it faster, but his ankle was holding him back. If only their chain could resist their attack!

The shutters were closed, it was probable that no one was there. However, he rang. He always preferred to hand-deliver packages. It was safer. At first, during his first stops, he had been imprudent. Some customers had no hesitation in saying that they hadn't received their package when Nick had duly dropped it off at their doorstep. He listened, he had heard footsteps, then bolts being opened and finally, a little lady appeared. She had the silhouette of a child, but the head of an adult, with messy hair, her shapeless dress hadn't been washed in a long time. She smelled of dampness and dirty dog. Nick forced himself to smile.

"Hello Miss, how are you?"

She looked at him, she seemed surprised that the delivery man asked her this question, she stammered:

"Fine, thank you and you?"

"Well, thank you, here is your package. Have a good day!"

As he limped towards his truck, she called out to him:

"Hey! Wait a minute, let me give you something."

He retraced his steps; she handed him a five dollars bill. He said:

"You are sure? It's a lot."

"I see that you limp. You are brave and I am happy to receive my package at home. I have my old car, but given the time I haven't driven it, I don't even know if it would start."

Nick thanked her, wished her a nice day, then returned to his truck. He went not far from the dogs, he noticed that they remained quiet.

Sitting behind the wheel, he looked at the list of his upcoming stops. The day would be tough, it was going take a lot longer with that damn injury, but he had no choice. The doctor at the hospital had advised him not to return to work until he was completely recovered. *At least a fortnight's rest,* he had prescribed. As if it were possible! No job, no pay, and without pay, the landlady would throw them out, Sarah, him and the unborn baby. If there had been only Sarah and him, sleeping for a few weeks in a tent would have been possible, but with the baby who could point his nose at any time... It was out of the question... The gynecologist who followed the Sarah's pregnancy had scared them: *Be careful, Mrs Kowalski, it's very low, you can give birth early, rest...* At this thought, Nick gritted his teeth. He grumbled: *These medics, they give recommendations, but they don't know anything about our lives!*

Sarah had been unemployed since COVID erupted and no one would hire her in her condition. She could no longer conceal her belly and the baby must not arrive too soon. The words of the doctor kept coming back in his head: *Wait until he's eight months old, then he won't have any big problems, but before, it can have serious consequences. What would you do with a deaf or blind kid?*

Sweeping away these dark thoughts, Nick couldn't help but imagine a beautiful baby in perfect health. Despite all their problems, they were happy to become parents. He drove off. The traffic around him was getting denser. A few minutes later he arrived at stop number 2. He jumped out of the truck, an excruciating pain crossed him. With the picture of a chubby baby in mind, he had forgotten his ankle again. Grimacing, he grabbed the parcel, then he hopped on one foot to the door of a large, opulent house. He then realized that he had changed neighborhoods.

Mercy! What was happening to him? For the first time since he drove around this city, he had passed Saint Maria of Czestochowa without making the sign of the cross. It made him quite sad. He felt he had offended his ancestors who had come to Cicero from Poland and had fought with their whole community to build this church, testimony of their Catholic faith and their country of origin.

Immersed in his thoughts, he had forgotten that he had just rung, he jumped when he saw the customer appear:

"Hi!"

In front of him stood a man in his forties, in Bermuda shorts. His t-shirt barely concealed a prominent belly, he was wearing flip-flops. Nick handed him the package:

"Hi! Have a good day!"

"Thank you! You, too!"

The customer closed the door. No tip this time, but anyway with COVID, the tip had almost disappeared, as had the signature attesting that the parcel had been received by the recipient.

He returned to his truck, dragging his sick leg. He was already late, with 148 stops left. He was hot and thirsty. Sitting in his cabin, he slipped a painkiller into his mouth, grabbed his bottle of water, took a huge sip, nearly spat it out and choked. He coughed, caught his breath, wiped his mouth with the back of his sleeve.

His tour continued like this, stop after stop. Eight hours later, he was around Burbank, he had 50 stops left. He wondered how he could make it, then he thought of the baby and said to himself that yes, he would finish his tour, no matter what. Come on, if he, Nick Kowalski, hadn't been able to study beyond high school, his little Alan would and even beyond College. He found himself dreaming, Alan would live in one of those ultra-plush houses in Hinsdale, the posh town where he had been a high school student, there he would practice the profession of dermatologist and would earn a lot of money by rejuvenating old skins.

His child would have a happy destiny. One day he would set foot on the land of his ancestors and would address vague cousins back home: *Here I am! I made it, you need my help, my money is at your service.* He would create a foundation that would fund a help center for the poor and scholarships for students. That day would come, but until then it was up to him, Nick, his father, must do what was necessary.

He stuffed a pill, ate a banana and went on his way.

It was 11:30 p.m. when he finally got home. With Sarah, they lived in a tiny house in Willowbrook.

From the street, it was barely distinguishable. In fact, it was taken to be an extension of one of the two large residences that framed it, which was undoubtedly the case originally. He entered quietly and immediately noticed Sarah's breathing. Everything was fine, she had fallen asleep, she had not waited for him to return like so many other times when he had felt guilty of coming home so late. He took off his shoes, opened the fridge, took out a Polish yoghurt, added a large spoonful of cranberry jam, gulped it all down. He completed his collation with a painkiller, climbed the spiral staircase that gave him access to the room upstairs, which served as a bedroom. Sarah was sleeping soundly. He laid down beside her. He fell asleep immediately. His phone's alarm was set for six o'clock.

2
Hinsdale, Princeton Road

As the days passed, the hours away from Sarah seemed longer to Nick. However, things were getting better, he had recovered his ankle, his deliveries were less painful. The future mother had arrived at the fateful eight months so that Alan could be born without dangerous consequences.

Preparations for the baby's arrival were well advanced. Sarah had set up a corner of their room, where they would place the basket. Nick's grandmother, babcia Magda, who did not speak a word of English, had arrived from Poland to help them during the first weeks. She had brought a complete trousseau for her great-grandson: Embroidered linen, sheets and pillowcases, adorable and old-fashioned clothes: fine cotton shirts, adorned with lace, panties, pajamas, and baby's vests knitted in white wool, bibs embroidered with miscellaneous animals, and icing on the cake, which had made the future parents smile, old-fashioned diapers in thick terry cloth, accompanied by their safety pins. It was proof that disposable diapers had not yet completely replaced them in Poland.

The date of the baptism had been set, contrary to Nick's wish. The whole family was about to welcome the child. Sarah and Nick had managed to keep the secret as to the first name of child, despite pressure from both families. It was only among themselves that they dared pronounce the name of their child, accompanying it with their dreams... *Alan will do this, that. When Alan will be at university, we will pay him everything, he will only have to worry about his studies... We will have to keep an eye on him with drugs circulating everywhere... Above all, avoid him falling into this pitfall...*

Deep in thought, Nick realized he had passed his next stop. He stopped, looked at the screen of his GPS. That was right, he had to go back. The cars were already honking and trying to pass him. He had to continue to the next crossroads, make a U-turn, find the house indicated on the delivery address. He drove about five hundred yards, turned right and found himself on a less busy street. He parked his truck on the side, re-recorded the previous coordinates, as his GPS reacted as if the delivery had been done. He headed back to *Princeton Road*.

Arrived at the right address, he stopped the truck. He tried to seize the enormous parcel with his hands, realized that he could not carry it. He freed the hand truck, lowered the rear base of the truck, slid the package, then he wheeled the hand truck toward the thick row of trees that almost completely concealed the residence. He walked along the property for a few meters, discovered the garden path that led to the main door. A flash had sprung from a concealed camera, he understood that he was being filmed. On both sides of the path, the lawns mowed, cut short, were of an almost artificial raw green. He experienced a terrible desire to tread the grass with his bare feet. Now that he was near the facade, he discovered the swimming pool and saw the tennis court. He approached the house, sought to locate the doorbell, when he realized the door was ajar. His eyes bulged at what he had before him. He dropped his devil and exclaimed:

"O zesz kurwa![1]"

He stepped back. His heart raced. He put his hand to his chest, closed his eyes for a moment, he had to overcome his emotion, face it. What was that? He forced himself to reopen his eyes. He made out a bare foot whose sole was pink and the top dark, but if he saw the sole... it was that... Arming himself with courage, he pushed the door open. His throat tightened till he couldn't articulate, not even a curse.

A woman... She was lying full length, her dress lifted, revealing her panties. Several red spots had formed on her chest and had pierced her clothes.

Trembling in horror, Nick was invaded by a multitude of confused thoughts. He was totally distraught. What should he do? Call his manager? Notifying the emergency services, the police? But then, what would become of him? How long had she been lying there without anyone noticing? He didn't dare come closer to her, he should see if her blood was fresh, if her heart was still beating... But he could also simply leave. Another one would come sooner or later...

---

1 *Holy shit,* in polish.

Such were his thoughts when he remembered the flashes of the cameras that he had perceived on his arrival between the row of trees and the door of the home. He had undoubtedly been filmed. Moreover, it would be easy to identify him since his truck, too, may have been filmed. If he ran away, he would be found very quickly and – absolute horror - suspected of the assault... whereas if he stayed and waited for the neighborhood police, he could explain himself. It was then that he heard the crying of a baby coming from above. He was not alone in the house with the woman's body. A baby... My God... he signed himself several times and hesitated no longer.

He pulled out his cell phone and feverishly typed in the emergency number, 9-1-1. Someone replied immediately:

"Hello, I'm listening, what's your problem?"

"It's not me, I'm fine, but there's a woman next to me, she's lying down, she does not move."

"Is she dead? Hurt? Is she losing her blood?"

"I don't know, I dare not look."

"Give me the address."

"Princeton Road No..."

"OK, I'll send you the emergency doctors. Above all, stay calm, they will be with you in an instant."

Nick heard the click that ended the call. He held his phone for a few more seconds in his hand. He felt exhausted, yet he was far from having finished his tour. What was going to happen? The rescuers were going to hold him, ask him questions. What could he answer them? He knew nothing of what had happened. He didn't know anything about this woman. Was she the mother of the crying child?

The child... He had forgotten to tell them about the baby. Somebody had to take care of this child whose tears redoubled in intensity. To reach the floor above, he would have to step over the body... It was out of the question! He didn't have long to wait, help was coming, they would do what was required. He tried to think about the problem of his package. He had no one to give it to. He looked on his cell phone for the phone number left by the customer when ordering. He typed it. Bullshit! The telephone was ringing here, very close to him, on the black marble slabs, beside the woman.

He heard the emergency car alarm, left the house to wave to them. He pushed aside the hand truck with the parcel lying on it, what was he going to do with it? Should he leave it in the house or return it to the warehouse?

The two-person rescue team rushed into the house. In a turn of hand, they loaded the woman onto the stretcher, installed an injection syringe, performed a first cardiac massage. They talked together without considering the presence of Nick:

"She looks very badly off, this poor woman! We might be able to save her, but we must act very quickly! She received several stab wounds; we must call the police and ask the delivery man to wait for them. We must take her to the hospital immediately. We will continue the massage in the ambulance."

Nick took advantage of the fact that they were busy to walk away with his hand truck, but one of the rescuers caught up with him:

«Hey man, don't go! We are taking the woman to the hospital, but you must wait for the police, we warned them, they will be here in a few minutes."

Nick felt trapped. Of course, he knew he was only a witness, but the woman had received several stab wounds. Perhaps when he arrived, his attacker was still around? In the house, in the thickets, nearby? Come on, come on, he had to keep his head cool, he too could have been filmed, so, no reason to panic, the police would find him. Just after the emergency services left, he heard the roar of the sirens. The tires of two cars squealed on the black tarmac, the doors slammed. Two minutes later, three uniformed police walked up the aisle. As they approached, one of them called out to Nick:

"Hey, man! Did you find the body?"

"Yes, I was delivering this package. The door was open, there was her foot."

"Whose foot?"

"Of the woman."

"Her name?"

"I do not know. I do not know her."

"Well, if you brought a package, it means that a customer ordered it, so who is it, what is the name of this client?"

"Yes, sorry, I'm upset. That's Mr. Edward P. Smith."

The policeman exclaimed:

"Oh fuck! EPS, it falls on us. It may be a source of trouble... Worth its bundle of dollars! Guys, you gotta watch out!"

The policeman turned to the delivery man:

"Well, then, you, when you arrived to deliver your package, the door was open. Where was the woman exactly?

"There, lying in the hallway, with her foot in the door. I didn't touch anything. I called 911 immediately. The paramedics said they could save her, they took her straight to the hospital. So, I forgot to tell them about the baby I heard crying upstairs.

"A baby? Is there a baby here? Where?

"Well, I do not know, upstairs probably, I tell you."

One of his colleagues, a big burly man with a protruding belly and a boxer's neck, went near Nick, grabbed the collar of his polo shirt, squeezed it. Nick gasped; his breath suddenly cut off. He felt the cop's boozy breath on his face.

"So, you heard crying, huh, but I thought you had just arrived!"

Nick couldn't answer, he was half choked, he was starting to feel bad, he collapsed on the floor.

"Hey Jojo, what the hell are you doing? Leave him alone! It's just the delivery boy. You are going to make a bloody mess again!"

"No, that one is not colored, we risk nothing."

"Stop talking bullshit, I tell you he did nothing but bring his package. Good, tell the owner of the house that his wife was assaulted."

He went to Nick, helped him up."

"What's up mate? Excuse him, he doesn't always know how to restrain himself. Listen, you need to call your client, you're going to tell him that the police are at his house and you're going to ask him to come right away, do you understand?"

Nick swallowed his saliva with difficulty, his throat hurt. He tried to articulate:

"I did, but it was this phone next to the woman that rang. Can you see, it is still on the ground."

"Do you have another number you could call?"

"I don't think so, but I'll check the order form.

Nick took the slip that had remained in his pocket. There was another number. He composed it, a man replied:

"Edward Paul Smith speaking, who's calling me?"

"Hello Mr. Smith, I am the delivery man for Pigeon Transport. I am in front of your house with your package, but I have no one to leave it with. What should I do with it?"

"Well, what, you dare disturb me for a delivery? I will complain of your incompetence to Pigeon Transport! Well, leave it to Mrs. Smith, the lady you found at my home, she is my wife."

"But well ... Wait, I'll put you through to the police who are there."

"Hello, Mr. Smith. Sorry, I have bad news for you. Your woman was attacked, she is injured, and she was transported by ambulance to the hospital."

"And Ray? Where is Ray?"

"Who is Ray?"

"You must come right away."

"I am too far. I will ask my sister to come. Can you wait for her?"

"Not easy, we have already been called to another site."

"One of you should stay put. I warn my sister, she lives nearby, she is certainly at home. It will take her a few minutes to arrive, she can take care of the little one. For my part, I will go to the hospital in Hinsdale where they probably took my wife."

"OK. And the delivery man, what should he do with your package?"

"Leave it there, it's an order."

"Very well, goodbye, Mr. Smith."

The policeman addressed Nick:

"Okay, man, order from Edward Paul Smith, you leave the package at the house."

Then to his colleague:

"Rob, you stay here, you wait for Mr. EP. Smith's sister."

Back to Nick:

"You, the delivery man, you can go, but leave us your name, telephone, address, number of your truck. You'll have to come to the Hinsdale station to give your statement."

Nick handed over one of the business cards he had on him, it contained his contact details. He could leave now, but he felt very tired, as if he had just completed 6 days of delivery... In addition, his left arm was painful, he must have hurt himself when he fell because of the policeman who had so violently jostled him... He rolled the hand truck, slid the package to the back of the entrance, nodded to the police and walked away. His throat was so tight that he was unable to make a sound.

He returned to his truck, started the engine, went into automatic mode, trusting his guidance system. Whatever happened would happen, he was too exhausted to think and certainly to make decisions.

3
ON THE SOUTH ROAD

Fortunately, Nick knew this southern route well. He had just driven along Midway Airport. He began to relax, turned on his favorite radio station, a station dedicated to jazz. Luckily, he came across the replay of the Chicago Jazz Festival. He smiled, happy memories flooding. Nights spent in Grand Park with his friends, listening, but also playing. He had learned sax by himself.

Now the radio was playing *Superstition,* one of the first songs he had managed to get out of his instrument, after rehearsing a simplified version for hours on end... The last notes vanished and gave way to an advertisement praising the merits of the Goose Island IPA 35[2]. Nick realized he was very thirsty, he felt the passenger seat, couldn't find his water bottle there. Unable to stop to look for it, he ran his tongue over

---

2 IPA 35 is one of the beers produced by the Goose Island Beer Company, a Chicago-based craft brewery.

his lips and swallowed his saliva. Throwing one eye outside, he noticed that night had fallen. He chased the music out of his head and turned off the radio. Concentrating on the denser traffic, he had only one idea in mind: Get home as soon as possible. Sarah must have been waiting impatiently for him. He had thought of telling her of his delay, but after reflection, he had preferred not to do so, because he would have had to provide him with the reason; and it seemed inconceivable to him, given her condition, to evoke the bloody body of this woman lying in the entrance of her residence. He sighed and accelerated to get into the right lane.

A fine rain had started to fall, the wind had picked up. He could no longer clearly distinguish the vehicles which preceded him. Suddenly, in front of him, he heard an enormous crash. He tried to slow down slamming on the brakes, but it was too late. In a last effort to avoid the pile-up, he gave a violent turn of the steering wheel which veered the truck on the right. The front of the vehicle crashed into the safety barrier and came to a stop.

Very shaken, Nick did not react immediately. He realized he had avoided the worst. If he had not had this life-saving reflex, he would have been caught in the huge pile of scrap metal he could make out on his left, he would probably be dead... His windshield had exploded, screams burst out everywhere, it was urgent to get out of the way as quickly as possible. He put on the gloves that he used to handle the parcels, brushed away the broken glass from his yellow jacket, then he unblocked his seatbelt. He twirled his arms and wiggled his legs. Apparently, he had nothing broken.

He tried to open the door of his truck, but the shock had deformed it. He repressed the dizziness that invaded him and folding the back of the passenger seat, he went to the back of the empty truck. He slid the bolt that blocked the big door, pushing back the leaves. He jumped on the tar and reached the safety zone behind the rail that bordered the highway.

He called the emergency accident number, then notified his company. The first question his manager asked him was whether he had completed his deliveries. It was only when he replied in the affirmative and confirmed that the truck was empty that she condescended to enquire about his health. She ordered him to stay until the tow truck arrived. She assured him that she would call someone she worked with on this stretch of road.

Nick felt the pain all over. He tried to stretch his muscles to reduce his tension. He was terribly thirsty, but his water bottle was out of reach, it was in the truck, and going there to retrieve it was out of the question. He looked down the road. Not far from him, the situation was a nightmare, the ambulances had come the opposite way, Nick saw the storm lanterns and the reflective bands of the rescuers wave behind the curtain of rain. He was safe.

Admittedly, his truck was out of order, but he was safe and sound. The tow truck would have a hard time to get to him. In any case, it would take a long time. He had to contact Sarah, because she was certainly riveted on the television news which reported the gigantic pileup. She may even be watching the crash footage, as several drones were now circling above his head in a hellish round. He perceived the flashes thrown by their cameras. She was going to panic when she recognized his truck... Sheltering his cell phone as best he could from the rain, he pressed her contact. He let it ring for a long time, then he started to worry, she didn't answer. Would she have gone to the hospital?

That's what he was thinking when the man from the convenience store introduced himself by his first name, Ben. He asked him to confirm his identity. Nick indicated his surname and first name, Kowalski, Nick, delivery man at Pigeon Transport. The man checked the corresponding boxes on his smartphone. Then he photographed the truck from all accessible angles, sent the information to Pigeon transport. Then he motioned to Nick to follow him. They skirted the security barrier and they found themselves a hundred meters further on, on an access ramp. Ben got him into his tow truck. He took out a sheaf of slips, had them filled and signed by Nick. The repairman said to him:

"I'll drop you off at home. I will return to take charge of the evacuation of the truck."

Nick didn't answer, he felt drained, without strength. He was very worried about Sarah. He couldn't wait to get home and hug her. Twenty minutes later they were in front of his house, Nick thanked Ben and got out of the truck. The repairman left right away.

Nick took out his key and slipped it into the lock. He didn't have to turn it; the door wasn't locked.

What had happened? The house was abnormally quiet. Usually, Sarah kept a musical background, or the news purred on the television. Horribly distressed, he climbed the small staircase as quickly as possible, their bed was empty. Doubt was no longer possible, Sarah had gone to the hospital. Tears blurred his vision, he felt guilty, he had failed to keep his word. He had promised her that he would be there to hold her hand during her delivery.

He passed his forearm over his eyes, went down again before calling the maternity ward. He asked if Sarah Kowalski had been admitted, the answer having been affirmative, he left and went to his parking lot to take his car. When he arrived at the hospital, he had to put on a cosmonaut outfit and go through a disinfectant airlock before being allowed into the delivery room. A midwife led him to Sarah. Her eyes were closed, her features drawn. He gently took her hand, caressed it and said:

"Excuse me, I'm late, but I..."

Sarah did not reproach him for his absence, she contented herself with saying with a faint smile:

"There are three of us now, you can ask to see him, Alan is in the observation room with other newborns. I was told that I was going to be installed in a room within a few minutes. Tomorrow, if all goes well, we can go home."

Nick's eyes stung, salty tears welling up. Fortunately, the midwife came back to them, she helped Sarah into a wheelchair, then she accompanied them to the room. Nick took Sarah in his arms; he laid her between the cool sheets. He went into the toilet, wetted a washcloth with cold water, wiped it over her face. He opened the briefcase Sarah had brought. It had been ready for more than a week, he took out a brush from the toilet bag. He untangled Sarah's hair, handed her a lavender-soaked handkerchief, then sat down, next to her on a chair. He forgot his pain. He glanced at the little bed intended for the baby, it was empty. Seized with fear, he imagined that the truth had been hidden from them and that their baby was dead. He got up abruptly, whispered in Sarah's ear:

"I am going to see my son!"

She smiled without opening her eyes and dozed off.

Nick left the room, closing the door softly. He walked down the hall to the office of the midwives.

He called out to the woman in a white coat who had her eyes riveted on her computer:

"I would like to hug my son."

She looked at him over her glasses:

"Who are you?"

"My name is Nick Kowalski; my wife has just given birth to a little boy."

"Okay, I'll take you there, but you cannot stay more than a few minutes, because the post-birth examinations are not over. You will be able to enjoy it more when you'll be at home. Have you applied for paternity leave?"

"No, even if I have the right according to the Law, I don't have the means."

"Your company doesn't pay you?"

"Nope."

The woman got up; she guided him to the room reserved for newborns. She went to a small transparent plastic bed. The first and last names of the child were written on a label:

"There you are, your son: Alan, Nick, Donald Kowalski."

She lifted the baby at arm's length, then handed it to Nick.

"Support his head, he cannot do it on his own, but he will do it quickly. He is in perfect health. Its weight, eight pounds, is perfect. Now, his hair is brown, but he will lose them, you will find out his real hair color in a few weeks. Given its skin color, very pale, there is a chance that he will turn blond or red."

Nick felt invaded by an indefinable feeling, a mixture of happiness, tenderness, intense emotion... and especially of gratitude towards Sarah who offered him this marvelous gift. For a moment, he forgot everything else. He would have stood there, stuck for hours if the midwife hadn't spoken to him:

"So how does it feel to become a dad?"

"It's the first time, I'm a little scared, I really want him to be happier than me, to make his life less hard than mine. I will do everything for that. His mother and I, we would like him to become a great doctor."

While saying those words, imagining his son's future, Nick remembered his high school days, when he was mocked by the children of the bourgeois of Hinsdale, he the child of Willowbrook.

Certainly, he went to this school with the other young people of his neighborhood, the high school of the rich, but he did not belong to their social environment. He had tried to join them thanks to his good school results, but he had to work to finance his studies, he had not succeeded. His son would be one of the privileged. He would justify all the sacrifices he and Sarah were willing to make.

Despite the late hour of the night, the midwife was smiling. The years passed, but she never tired of seeing the joy of fathers, when there was one, in front of their child. She said:

"I'm sure you'll get there. We are in the United States, the country where anything is possible. Me, you see, my mother arrived, a very young widow, from Vietnam with me and my sister. We were very small. She took any job, and we were both able to complete good training. I became a midwife, and my sister works in a bank. You'll see, everything will be fine for your little Alan."

Nick's shoulders dropped; his body finally relaxed. A feeling of pure happiness invaded him. He thanked this woman who seemed older than him, a little younger than would have been. his mother if she had been alive.

A few minutes later, the midwife took the baby from him to put him back in his crib, then she led the new father down the hall.

4

Hinsdale, Police Station

After his visit to the hospital, Nick had collapsed on his bed. It's the alarm of his cell phone which woke him up. He rubbed his eyes. What time was it? Half past seven. He should have been at the depot at seven o'clock. He called Pigeon Transport, explained his situation as a new father. He was generously given three days off, but unfunded. Despite the loss of income, he decided to take them. During the day, he had to get Sarah and her son back home, because one more day in the hospital would ruin them.

He phoned the maternity ward to get news and find out at what time he could fetch them. The person who answered him, a man for once, told him that Sarah and the baby were going to be visited by the doctor. If all went well, they could leave the maternity ward at noon. Anyway, the room had to be vacated by 1 p.m. at the latest, otherwise he would pay an extra day. Nick assured him that he would be there at noon.

He took advantage of the morning to fill the refrigerator as well as the pantry of the kitchenette. Sarah would have what she needed when he went back to work. He had just come back with his big bags; he had started to tidy up when his phone rang.

"Nick Kowalski?"

"Yes, it's me."

"We expect you at Hinsdale Police Station today. You will have to deposit your testimony regarding the Princeton Road assault."

Nick felt his throat constrict and he could not answer, so his interlocutor insisted:

"You understand correctly, don't you? Come as soon as possible."

Nick pulled himself together, he replied in one go:

"Yes, I understand. I won't be able to come before two o'clock, because I have to pick up my wife and my son in the maternity ward."

"Ah… OK, congratulations."

Nick heard the end of communication click. He felt oppressed, he knew Hinsdale police station, which only brought back very bad memories. A theft story and a drug one came back to him.

On several occasions, he had been summoned with comrades at 121 Symonds Drive.

Strangely enough, they all lived in Willowbrook, while the wealthy kids of Hinsdale had not been bothered. Yet, some of them took drugs and were dealing. Two had even died of overdose. He murmured: *Justice, we should rather speak of Injustice...*

He felt an icy shiver run down his spine. What were they going to ask him? A testimony... But if they needed a culprit, he would be the ideal culprit. He started to think, he shouldn't let them go ahead... Going alone to the police station would put him in danger... Methodically, he reviewed his former high school classmates. Luckily, they had had a reunion of former students a few weeks before and some of them were already well advanced in their professional careers. Rupert Isaiah Kantorowicz's name came up, He was a young lawyer, he had recently opened his practice in Chicago.

Nick feverishly looked for the number on his laptop. He called him and luckily, he got him on the line; after introducing himself, he spoke in one breath:

"Hello Rupert, I got into a dirty business. As I told you at the meeting, I am currently a delivery driver for Pigeon Transport. Yesterday, during a delivery, I found myself in the home of a woman who had just been assaulted. I have been summoned today to Hinsdale station to testify, but I'm afraid the police will make life easier for them by putting me in prison."

"Well, hello Nick. So yesterday, when you were delivering a package to a customer, what happened exactly?"

"When I reached my place of delivery, a superb villa on Princeton Road, in Hinsdale, the door was ajar. A lifeless woman was lying on the ground. After several minutes during which I remained unable to do anything, I was in such a shock, I alerted the emergency services. They arrived very quickly and took the woman away. The police came next. A policeman made the first observations, he told me that I should come and testify at the police station. This morning I didn't have time to do it and now I must go to the

maternity ward, fetch my wife and my son. A policeman from Hinsdale station just called me to tell me
again that I absolutely had to go there today. I don't
think it would be safe to go there by myself. Would
you be available to accompany me?"

Rupert I. Kantorowicz gave himself time for
reflection. Alan didn't have a penny, but maybe he had
a good insurance in case of disputes? Furthermore,
it was certain that Pigeon Transport, a company that
had a storefront, had no interest in seeing one of its
delivery men accused of homicide...

He replied:

"Give me an hour, I'll call you back."

"Thank you, I'm counting on you."

Rupert I. Kantorowicz rubbed his hands, he
was a little out of cases and there, he saw a business
that could pay well if he knew how to maneuver.
He immediately phoned the Pigeon Transport legal
department:

"Hello, here, Rupert I. Kantorowicz, lawyer in
Chicago. Can you put me to the person who settles
disputes between deliverers and customers?"

A few minutes later, he had a correspondent from
the legal department:

"Hello, Reginald County, what is your problem?"

Rupert explained to him the situation in which
his client, Nick Kowalski, found himself. He argued
the risks incurred by the company if a delivery person
were to be charged. His interlocutor replied laconi-
cally:

"We will have no problem; we have an excellent
contract with American Insurance. I'll let them know,

they'll appoint a lawyer who will take charge of the case."

"Perfect. For my part, I intend to defend the personal interests of Nick Kowalski. Would you kindly send me the contact details of your lawyer so that I can get in touch with him."

"OK, it will be done, leave me your email address, it will be more convenient."

Rupert gave it to him, then he thanked him and took his leave. He then called Nick back.

"Well, I agree to take charge of your defense. First, I will accompany you to Hinsdale Police Station. Knowing your financial situation, I will not ask you anything for the moment. Thereafter, if necessary, we will draw up a contract specifying my commitment as well as my pay."

"Thank you, Rupert! I am so grateful to you."

"Please, it's only natural to help each other among old high school friends and besides, pals of the Polish community. Let's meet at two-thirty at the Corner Bakery in Hinsdale. We will agree on how we are going to present your testimony. Above all, don't call me by my first name when we're at the station, but Doctor Kantorowicz or simply Doctor. As of today, I am your representative with the police and justice, I'm not your old high school friend anymore."

"Okay, I'll be vigilant, thank you again. See you soon."

Nick felt relieved. Assisted by Rupert, he did not risk ending up behind bars, at least for now. However, if he wanted to be on time at the Bakery, he had to hurry, because he had first to pick up Sarah and little Alan from the maternity ward. It was eleven thirty.

He rushed to the hospital. He went to reception desk, asked for the bill since he wanted to pay before looking for Sarah and the baby, but this was denied. He was obliged to go to the room occupied by his wife to make sure that the doctor who had examined them in the morning agreed to let them go, then he returned to pay and finally got his wife and child back. Sarah was tired, she had slept badly. She had shadows around her eyes, but she did not complain. She guessed that Nick was stressed, she put his nervousness on the account of his very recent status as a father.

At home, Nick helped her transfer the baby and their stuff in the bedroom. He left after checking that she had everything she would need within easy reach. Besides, he had warned his grandmother. She would come in the afternoon and all the more easily since he had given her a duplicate key to the front door.

Nick arrived a little early for his meeting with his lawyer. He ordered a coffee at the counter, then moved to the back of the Corner Bakery, to watch for Rupert's arrival. It wouldn't be difficult; it was no longer time for lunch and teatime had not started.

The lawyer walked through the door at the agreed time, 2:30pm. Nick waved at him. Rupert sat down across from him. A few seconds later, the waitress took their order. Nick, who hadn't eaten nothing since breakfast, chose a huge sandwich with bacon, eggs, cheese, onions, tomatoes, and salad. Rupert Isaiah settled for a double coffee spread with whipped cream. He let Nick swallow half his sandwich before addressing the issue that brought them together.

"Okay, Nick, tell me exactly what happened, taking the facts in the order in which they occurred."

Nick recounted his arrival in the street of the residence, the difficulty experienced in detecting the door of the house, then this unimaginable scene of the woman lying down.

"What did the rescuers do?"

"They tried to revive the woman, I heard them, they said they could save her, they took her away very quickly after notifying the police and telling me to wait for them, which I did."

"What did you tell the police?"

"Exactly what I just told you, that I was there for the delivery."

"There were certainly cameras, there are always in this kind of luxury residence."

While saying these words, Rupert could not help but smile as he remembered his expedition in the upscale district of Hinsdale... He was thirteen years old; he had entered a house through the window of a toilet that was left open. Small and slender for his age, he edged his way in, then he made around the house. There was nobody. He still remembered his amazement at discovering the enormous screen and the musical equipment of the room in the basement. His visit had been interrupted by the sound of a shrill bell triggered by the alarm system. He silently rushed into the kitchen, swiped a bag of candy bars, and grabbed a camera, then he left as he had come. Hearing the police car sirens, he hid behind a thicket. He had seen the police enter the house, go around it and then leave... He still remembered the cramp that had almost blocked him when he had left his refuge.

He had never done it again, but he had never felt remorse either. He had chosen to become a criminal lawyer because he understood that when you were on the side of the poor, you might be tempted to rob those who were excessively rich and take a little of their surplus from them...

And now one of his old high school classmates found himself in a case that could be dangerous if the police did not quickly find the real culprit. He did not believe that Nick was a man capable of killing to appropriate what did not belong to him or else he had changed completely from the kid he had been. As a teenager, he was friendly, most often on the side of the weak. Rupert knew something about it, Nick had not hesitated to help him one day when he had found himself framed by three muscle men who wanted his skin. He had been grateful to him at the time and also afterwards, because his attackers had left him alone. Nick was feared. He was tall and very strong for his age. He had remained so because to work as a delivery man at Pigeon Transport, you had to be super strong!

"Nick, I was thinking back to our high school days. I would like to know why you have me defended at the time?"

Nick was very surprised by the question. Certainly, he had come to his aid in the past, but it was a long way off. He opened his mouth, not knowing what he could answer, then the words spoken by Father Ambrozy Bovery who ensured his religious formation during his high school years came back to him: *The Law of Christ is simple: Love one another, stand up for the weak and you will win the heaven.*

He answered very simply:

"I strive, despite the difficulties of life, to remain faithful to my education. As you certainly know, within our Catholic community, religion holds a great place. I practice as much I can, given the time the work leaves me. It's not always easy, because I have fluctuating schedules, I work on Sundays and even when I get ahead of my deliveries, it is not rare that instead of complimenting me, my manager adds additional work. I know that if I refused, my evaluation would suffer."

"Are you evaluated?"

"Constantly, by my supervisor, by the clients, by the robotic system that tracks us down during our moves."

"How do you see the future? Are you going to stay at Pigeon Transport?"

"I'm not thinking about the future right now. I have to feed my family, I just had a child, my wife is unemployed, and she has to rest because she gave birth yesterday."

"Oh, congratulations! What's it like to be a father?"

Nick smiled, it was the second time he had been asked that question in 24 hours, first the midwife and now his lawyer.

"I'm moved. My goal is to ensure a better future than mine for my son. I am ready to do anything for it."

"Even to kill?"

Nick was amazed. Incredulous, he looked at Rupert. It took him some time to produce an answer in a broken voice:

"Do you think I'm guilty?"

"No, I said that for fun. If I thought you guilty of a crime, I wouldn't have accepted to defend you because I know that I would have had no chance of winning your case if a day there were a trial. Well, fortunately, we are not at that end. Let's resume. Later, I will be speaking to the police, I will tell them the facts as you have reported them. Anyway, they also have the testimony of the rescuers and what is very positive as far as you are concerned is that you did not flee, because you could have fled."

"I thought about it, after realizing that the woman had just been assaulted, I was panicked. I thought about running away, but I noticed the flash of a camera, I realized that I had been filmed. Besides, my truck was parked in front of the house, it bears the name of my company painted on the body in huge letters. They would have found me, so I stayed. I reassure myself telling me that the real aggressor was certainly filmed too."

"Speaking of him, you did not notice anything in particular? You didn't see a shadow slipping away, you wouldn't have spotted a trace of the assailant?"

"No, I was too shocked to perceive anything."

"I'll ask for the images of the cameras, there may be something to get out of it. In any case, they will support your testimony."

"Yes, you're right, it's a good idea."

"Well, if you agree, let us go."

Nick stuffed the rest of his sandwich in his mouth, finished his glass of fountain soda, then he took out his card, but Rupert Isaiah Kantorowicz stopped him with his hand:

"Leave it, it's for me. I invite you, it's the least I can do to celebrate the birth of your son."

An idea crossed Nick, he asked:

"Would you agree to be his godfather? Unless you already have children?"

"No, I don't have children and I'm not sure I want any, but you forget that I could not be his religious godfather, I'm not catholic, I'm jewish."

"Ah yes, it's true, but you could be his secular godfather. You could show him the way of successful people, you would be a role model for him."

Rupert looked at his old comrade. He had remained naive, he still believed in grand sentiments. He had kept moral principles despite being taken advantage of by his company. However, we were in the United States, the success of an individual was measured not by the quality of his soul, but by the contents of his bank account. Rupert suddenly took pity on Nick. If he didn't help him, he would be crushed by the system. The image of Charlie Chaplin caught in the infernal machine of modern times, came back to him. Nick's face replaced the actors. He would have to fight for him. He would do it and not just for his personal advantage. He got up and said:

"It's time, Nick, do you feel ready?"

Nick gave him a confident look that touched what remained of his heart. He wouldn't tell him the real reason that made him accept his defense.

They left the Corner Bakery and headed for the police station.

Nick's throat was tight as he stepped through the doorway. His lawyer understood this and gently squeezed his shoulder. It is in this position that they presented themselves at the reception desk. Rupert Kantorowicz asserted in an authoritative voice:

"Hello Sir. My client, Nick Kowalski and myself, Rupert Kantorowicz, his lawyer, have an appointment with Christopher Flores."

"I will tell him. Please wait."

They moved away from the counter a little. A few minutes later, Christopher Flores fetched them and took them to his office. While Nick expected to be questioned about the facts surrounding the attack on the victim of the Princeton Road, the policeman began by giving them startling information on the facts of the case:

"The situation is not turning out at all as I expected. I got confirmation that the victim is not the wife of Mr. Edward P. Smith. Her name is Rosa Williams. She is nurse for the agency of Nurses Chicago services. On the day of the assault, Mrs. Smith asked the agency to send her a babysitter at noon sharp. As if the facts were not complex enough, Mr. Smith told us that his wife could not be found. She has disappeared. It is unknown when, but she did not reappear after leaving her home, a few minutes after the arrival of the nurse. She does not answer phone calls and she did not leave any information with any of her relatives. Alright, let's get to what you did that day. Who was in the house when you arrived?"

"I only saw that colored woman; I thought it was Mrs. Smith. She was lying on the ground, I thought she was dead and called for help. They came and got her to the hospital. In the meantime, they had notified the police and asked me to wait for them, which I did."

"At what time did you arrive at the house?"

"A few minutes after noon. I did not look then at the time."

"Did you really not see anyone? Yet, according to the images captured by the cameras placed in the garden and around the house, we can distinguish the assailant fully dressed in black. Five or six minutes later, you're there. It seems difficult, even impossible that you did not see him, especially since the cameras did not film him after you, which means he was in the house at the same time as you."

"No, I haven't seen anyone but this woman. Then I heard the baby cry."

"You didn't go to see that child? You hear him cry and you do not try to give him help?"

"The paramedics arrived very quickly, then the police."

The lawyer intervened:

"Mr. Flores, my client was there to deliver a package. Imagine the shock he suffered when he arrived at his client's home and discovered the victim. Let us admit it's an unusual scene, fortunately. I find that his reaction in alerting the emergency services was completely appropriate. As for the videos, you will communicate them to me, I will watch them because in this case, timing is everything. That said, I don't see what the interest of my client would be to deny having seen the aggressor, quite the contrary."

"He could have made a deal with him, like: You don't say anything, and I'll pay you a good sum."

"Mr. Flores, my client has an irreproachable past. I vouch for his honesty. My client has never taken drugs, he has never been convicted or even suspected of any crime whatever. One does not become a criminal overnight and even so, what would be his interest in attacking this woman? He was only there to deliver goods."

"As for today, I am willing to believe in the innocence of your client. Mr. Nick Kowalski, you may leave. However, I ask you not to leave the State of Illinois and to stay available for any summons required by the investigation."

"It will be the case. My client absolutely does not seek to escape the investigation, he knows that he is an essential witness, and he accepts this fact. Goodbye Mr. Flores."

"Goodbye, gentlemen."

Nick felt real relief. As soon as they got out of the police station, he took a deep inspiration. His lawyer smiled:

"Come on, it was not so terrible. I'll let you go home on your own and I will go back to my office. See you soon and keep your spirits up. Hugs to Alan."

"Thank you, Rupert, fortunately you were there, I think without you, I would have cracked."

"I'm here for that, so that you feel supported, it's the role of a lawyer ... and a friend. Now that we're out of the police station, I can tell you that I'm both. Good way back."

5
SUSPICIONS

The day following Nick Kowalski's statement, Christopher Flores was already regretting not putting Nick Kowalski behind bars. After a night spent tossing and turning the news concerning the timing of the successive events on Princeton Road, it seemed to him impossible that the delivery man did not meet the aggressor, given the very short time that had elapsed between the arrival of the assailant and that of the delivery man.

He reached his office very early. In order to verify that his opinion was based on reality rather than his imagination, he immersed himself in the photos and videos taken by the cameras of the residence of EP Smith. They were many. They showed an individual dressed in a black tracksuit, with the face concealed by a mask. It was even impossible to make out his eyes, because he wore dark glasses. He was alone, his gloved hands were free of any object.

He was shown to arrive in front of the property, enter the house, then unfortunately, he there were no pictures of what happened inside. The murder weapon, a very sharp Laguiole knife intended for the cutting of meat, had been found in the kitchen, covered with the blood of the victim, but bearing no trace of the assailant. The cameras had recorded the coming of Nick Kowalski and the images confirmed his statement. They were not only dated, but the time of the shots was indicated.

Exactly five minutes had elapsed between photos of the assailant and the first ones of the delivery man.

The reexamination of the photos confirmed the opinion of Christopher Flores. He was convinced that Nick Kowalski had seen the murderer.

It was on this suspicion, despite the intervention of his lawyer, that he decided to send Nick Kowalski to court. For that, he had to arrest him. He was in a hurry to get it over with, so, he had to put pressure on the delivery man to make him admit having seen the assailant, even possibly admitting his complicity.

Once Nick Kowalski was arrested at home, he was transferred to court where he was immediately heard by the magistrate. Faced with the denials of the young man, the latter let him simmer in a cell for twenty-four hours. After this time, he expected a confession, but the delivery man maintained his testimony, not changing one iota of it, despite the harsh conditions of detention and the despair of being away from loved ones. The magistrate still restrained him, convinced that the delivery man would give in. However, he had underestimated the activism of Dr

Kantorowicz as well as the support that the young man was going to collect.

As soon as he learned of his client's arrest, the lawyer assisted him during his hearings. After the magistrate's decision to keep him in detention, Rupert I. Kantorowicz contacted his employer, Carrier Pigeon. This time, he did not ask to speak to the head of the legal department, he called the boss, Gerald Casper, directly. During their exchange, he put forward two shocking arguments:

"Thank you, Mr. Casper, for taking me on the phone. You know the situation of your employee, Nick Kowalski, whose defense I represent. However, what you may not know are the consequences of his arbitrary arrest. Your business could be hit hard by the media frenzy. If you have listened to the major news channels, you may have heard that they have begun to distill a flattering portrait of the young man who will soon make all generations weep. Nick Kowalski is described as serious, very well integrated, deserving, courageous, with an irreproachable past, married to a young woman unemployed because of the COVID and father of a newborn. Twenty-four hours after the arrest of Nick Kowalski, a demonstration in his favor was scheduled for Saturday. It is organized by the Polish community from Chicago and surrounding areas. The case is taking on dangerous proportions, it risks to represent very negative publicity for your company."

Gerald Casper tried to temporize:

"Mr. Kantorowicz, the media grabbed this piece of news, I admit, but their usual way of working will soon reassert itself. As soon as another news item takes place, the journalists will seize it, which will cause the disappearance of the Kowalski affair."

"Mr. Casper, let me insist, don't leave the situation as it is. I have some reliable information within the Polish community, to which I belong myself. Community mobilization is very strong. It would be necessary to lower the tension before Saturday. You certainly remember the riots that took place a few months ago. Not only will Nick Kowalski's supporters be very numerous, but they could find themselves largely supported by more violent groups that would cause disorder in the city. If so, the responsibility would fall on your business."

This time, the argument carried, because Gerald Casper recalled the images of the revolt which had followed the death of George Floyd. He could still see the looting of one of his warehouses as well as the ensuing arson. The lawyer was right, they had to find a way to close this negative episode. The boss of Pigeon Transport asked:

"Mr. Kantorowicz, I hear what you are saying, what would you advise me to avoid the situation flare up?"

"I intend to apply for my client's release on bail. On reflection, I think I can get it by posting $50,000 bail. Sure, I could collect this sum by launching a subscription, but that would take time and we don't have any. I could also get the sum from a bondsman[3], but I

---

3 The bondsman is a guarantor of judicial bail, the guarantor asks the accused to pay 6 to 20% of the sum, which the defendant will not recover. It is on this commission that the guarantor is remunerated. The defendant must

have small chances of getting there, because my client is not in a position to provide any compensation. The release of Nick Kowalski must be quick and publicized for the demonstration to be called off."

Gerald Casper no longer hesitated. It was better to pay the amount requested. The picture of the company would be preserved and even enhanced. This action would allow Pigeon Transport to appear as a humane company, concerned with the protection of its employees. That would be all the better because a union had just been created in one of its warehouses. This type of affairs, if left unresolved, would give subversive ideas to other employees.

"OK, you can already request the release of your client, I agree to pay the deposit. Send me your RIB, I will give the order to credit your account."

"Mr. Casper, thank you for your understanding. I am ready to act in conjunction with the legal department of your company, if necessary."

Gerald Casper smiled; this young lawyer was ambitious. Certainly, he had called him with the aim of defending his client, but he did not forget his personal interest...

---

also provide the bondsman with a security deposit, such as 40% of the bond in cash, or property with a value at least equal to the total due. In return, the guarantor submits to the court a contract by which he agrees to pay the deposit in the event that the defendant does not appear at the hearings. These contracts are most of the time financed by insurance companies capable of making the capital available quickly.

He contented himself with putting an end to the conversation. As soon as his appeal was over, the lawyer began the procedure of the request for release under bail. He had to do it very quickly. He went to court, laid siege to the magistrate, who finally received him the same day. He allowed himself to be convinced by his arguments. The next date of his renewal to his post was approaching.

The lawyer couldn't help thinking that this situation was no stranger to his assent. But no matter the true motivation of the magistrate, only his decision mattered. A few hours later, Nick Kowalski was free.

He immediately returned home. Sarah was taking a nap. His grandmother had already prepared dinner, he kissed her before advising her to leave. The first step he took was to call his manager to return to his job. Ann Pham replied:

"Hello Nick. I cannot decide alone. Personally, I am in favor of it, but I must refer to Adam. I'll let you know."

It was seven o'clock when finally, Ann Pham called him back:

"Adam doesn't want you to resume work now. Considering what you've been through, Pigeon Transport has decided to grant you a month's paid leave, take advantage of it. See you."

Nick couldn't believe it, he felt a mixture of joy, worry and disbelief. What was he going to do for the next 30 days? The house was very small. Sarah was assisted by his grandmother; she hardly needed him. He had the impression that doing nothing would be worse than everything. He was going to rehash the drama...

He informed his lawyer of Pigeon Transport's decision. Rupert I. Kantorowicz was not surprised. Indeed, he told him that this decision had been made in response to his request. Nick was a bit mortified, he replied that the least he could have done was for him to let him know.

6
ENTRANCE OF SAMANTHA GOSVENOR, FBI AGENT

The release of Nick Kowalski forced Christopher Flores to alleviate the pressure he exerted on the young man. He began to focus his research on the disappearance of Mrs. Stoica-Smith. Indeed, the young woman had still not given any sign of life. The examination of her telephone calls, obtained from her operator, indicated the recipient of her last call. This call was dated from the day of the attack, at noon. It was addressed to the Nurse services of Chicago, to request the sending of a person to take care of her child.

Christopher Flores had just received the recording of the call, he had listened to it several times. He wondered if it was really Mrs. Smith's voice. He decided to ask Edward P. Smith for his opinion. The latter had promised to come at the end of the afternoon. He was already seven o'clock. Christopher Flores sighed and whispered:

"These big shots think they're allowed anything. Make the police wait until no time? But no problem! If I ever dared to make a remark, this gentleman would be the person to answer me: *Now tell me, I'm the one who pays you, so if you're not happy, you quit, and I'll replace you!*"

Yes, except that the recruitment of new police officers was becoming more and more difficult. The candidates were no longer queuing up as before, the Chicago police and those of the neighboring towns had a bad reputation since several young men had been shot. People forgot that the police were the target of unscrupulous gangsters who did not hesitate to shoot. If they ever used their firearms, it was mostly out of fear of dying, murdered.

The police station clock struck eight. He got up and walked into the hall. The night shift had replaced the day shift. At the reception desk, Mario Collaccioni challenged him:

"Chris, incredible, are you still there?"

"I'm expecting Edward P. Smith."

"He gave you an hour or what?"

"No, he just promised he'd come to the station in the afternoon."

"Well, I pity you, this kind of individuals think anything is allowed. By the way, I heard that his wife has made a bunk, are you sure she wouldn't be an accomplice of his kidnappers? Has a ransom demand arrived?"

"To my knowledge, no, but Smith could have kept that to himself."

"I confirm. If he wants to get her alive, I think he better not put the police on it. Let's not forget that we are in Chicago, one of the great capitals of crime. For me, I've always lived here, I know how it works... What about you, where are you from?"

"Houston, Texas. My parents settled there when they were young."

"Oh yes, it's true, I thought you were a Mexicano."

"And you an Italo!"

Mario's chewing gum passed from one cheek to another to end up with a huge bubble that he made to burst. If he hadn't witnessed the scene, with the noise, Christopher could almost have imagined a small caliber bullet which had just been fired.

"Yah, but the Italians have been here much longer than the Mexicans. You, you are recent immigrants, not us."

"Yeah, but I think more of us are now originally Mexican than you originally Italians."

"We have more power. We no longer count our celebrities: Madonna, Fiorello La Guardia, Robert De Niro, Francis Ford Coppola, Nancy Pelosi, Frank Sinatra, Joe DiMaggio, Samuel Alito, Rudy Giuliani, Martin Scorsese, Enrico Fermi, Chris Botti while you, Mexicano..."

"You forget Jennifer Lopez, Alex Rodrigues, Benjamin Bratt..."

Christopher stopped quickly short, because to tell the truth, he had never looked into this question.

He added to compensate for the thinness of his list:

"Since Mexican immigration to the US is much more recent than the Italian one, it's normal that we have fewer celebrities, but you'll see, that will change very quickly. Besides, among Italo Americans, there are some very unsavory ones."

This time, Mario Collaccioni remained quiet. Christopher returned to his office. The police station was now closed to the public and silent.

Christopher Flores had dozed off when Mario Collacionni knocked on his door:

"Sorry to wake you up, but your visitor is here, he seems in a hurry."

Christopher stretched, ran his hand through his hair, then he rushed to meet Edward P. Smith.

"Good evening, Mr. Smith, thank you for coming."

"Good evening Mr. Flores, it's the least one can do."

Christopher led his visitor to his office at the end of the corridor, he ushered him in and invited him to sit down. Christopher was about to start recording when his visitor stopped him:

"Wait, there is more urgent. I refuse to be recorded because what I have to tell you is confidential. This afternoon, I received a ransom demand on my personal cell phone for the release of my wife. The sum is huge, I don't know if I will be able to collect it."

"This is a game-changer, it's very serious. The FBI should be notified immediately."

"What if I pay? The correspondent ordered me not to alert the police, on pain of sending back my wife cut into small pieces."

"Listen, Mr. Smith, let me call the FBI office in Chicago, at least get their opinion."

Edward P. Smith was extremely pale, he had lost his arrogance. He no longer seemed sure to leave the FBI out. Christopher took the opportunity to drive the point home:

"It is not uncommon that even in the event of payment of the ransom, the gangsters assassinate their victim for fear of seeing her testify against them."

"My wife is of Romanian origin; do you think that…"

He didn't finish his sentence, but Christopher, guessing what was left unsaid, turned it into an argument for FBI intervention:

"All the more reason to tell the FBI. They know the mafia networks. Kidnappings are a mode of extortion in full development. Did your wife move without protection?"

"Yes, she refused that I hire a bodyguard. It's silly, if I had imposed one on her, we wouldn't be there."

"It might be worse. I can't help linking the assault that took place at your home to the abduction of your wife. Since the gangster tried to kill the woman who was at your house, no doubt to avoid leaving behind him an embarrassing witness, he would not have hesitated to assassinate a bodyguard."

Edward P. Smith was silent for a long time. Christopher Flores was careful not to talk. He watched his visitor. His brow was furrowed, his gaze vague. He had to weigh the pros and cons against the intervention of the FBI.

"I hadn't interpreted the situation the way you do. I was convinced that the aggression of the nurse was the work of a prowler, possibly with the complicity of the delivery man. Your hypothesis leads me to give you my consent to involve the FBI. However, I ask you to keep the utmost secrecy. As you know, I am the head of an important financial company. If news of the ransom gets out, it could cause a collapse of my share price. My company would not be the only one concerned, finance is a castle of cards, a card falls and the whole building can topple over."

"You can trust me, I am not in the habit of talking to journalists. I can assure you that no information came from me in what the media broadcasted so far. In addition, the media mainly mentioned the delivery man, they barely mentioned your business name."

"It's true. I am grateful to you, especially since unhealthy rumors could jeopardize not only the price of my company on the stock exchange, but also the fortunes of thousands of people who have chosen my company to improve their assets."

With the approval of his interlocutor, Christopher dialed the number of his contact in the FBI, who was a former comrade of his, or rather a comrade who was first in their police academy's graduating class, then later switched to the FBI, Samantha Gosvenor.

He turned on the loudspeaker, the young woman's well-placed voice came clear:

"Hi! FBI Office, Samantha Gosvenor."

"Hi, Sam, Christopher Flores speaking, how are you?"

Samantha swallowed with difficulty... Chris... His voice... His voice which still took her to the guts, she could feel her belly calling out to her wildly. She managed, despite her emotion, to articulate a sentence in an almost normal way:

"Very well! What about you, Chris, how's it going in Hinsdale?"

"Not bad at all, I'm starting to make my mark. I meant to contact you since I heard you were assigned to Chicago. I thought we could meet again."

Sam didn't answer immediately. She was thinking. She knew that one day or another he was going to telephone, that he had evidently heard of her appointment in Chicago from one of their common acquaintances. Remembering the mind control instructions from the training given at the Quantico[4] academy, she succeeded in adopting a neutral tone:

"Well, I'm pretty busy, they put me in the scent at high speed. I am already responsible for a whole case."

"Listen, this is a more than urgent matter, I do not want to discuss it on the phone. Could you come by my office tonight?"

"This evening? You mean right now? But Chris, I'm already late, it's almost 9.pm."

"Sam, I really need your advice ASAP. Besides, I'm not only person to rely on you."

So, there was someone influential in Chris's office. Samantha thinks. Who could that be? Curiosity overcame her reluctance to see Christopher again. She yielded:

"OK Chris, I'll be there in forty-five minutes, time to leave the office and cover the distance."

---

4 Training center for FBI and Drug Enforcement special agents.

"Thank you, Sam, I'll make it up to you."

Samantha had hung up, she railed against herself. But in God's name why did I accept to go to Hinsdale? And first of all, what does he want from me, Chris?

Sam knew perfectly why she had acted like that; she was all the more mortified. She and Chris had a torrid affair when they were still law students, at the University of Austin. She felt the heat spread throughout her body and bit her lips violently. Her eyes were sparkling, she was going to resist him. At no price would she fall back into his net. It would be easier if he had married in the meantime? What was that story of not being able to seek his opinion by telephone?

She suddenly smiled; it came back to her that Chris was the lead investigator in the Smith case... It was certainly about this criminal case that he wanted her opinion... Something new must have cropped up, he needed the help of the FBI... If she refused, his request would be official. In this case, given her recent appointment, she would have no chance of winning the case, whereas if she was already involved, thanks to Christopher Flores, she would have the best assets to be appointed. Sam gathered her things. Going down to the parking lot of the building of the FBI, she decided that the relationship with Christopher Flores would be confined to work, no matter what. She had no desire to suffer as before. Relying on her resolution, she recovered her car. Thirty minutes later, she announced herself on the intercom of the Hinsdale police station, the door opened. She entered the hall. The reception orderly greeted her, told her that she was expected in the last office down the hall. She went there. The door was open. As soon as he saw her, Christopher jumped up and ushered her into the room, then closed the door behind her. He performed the introductions:

"Mr. Edward Peter Smith, this is Samantha Gosvenor, agent at the FBI office in Chicago."

Samantha shuddered inside, Edward P. Smith himself... It had to be serious... She was doubly disturbed, by the meeting with the illustrious boss and by the fact of seeing Chris. Her emotion was reflected in the smarting of the skin on her entire body. By a violent effort of will, she forced her brain to focus on what she knew about the Smith case.

Christopher did not leave her in suspense, he informed her of the ransom demand against the release of Mrs. Smith. She immediately asked E.P. Smith:

"Sir, do you have the recording of the request?"

Edward P. Smith replied:

"No, it was made through an application which was erased after the message was broadcast."

"What were you told?"

"The correspondent informed me that my wife was in their hands and that I would see her only after the payment of a ransom. Considering the amount of the sum demanded, I realized that I would not be able to raise the funds without resorting to a loan from my bank. So, I met my banker who assured me of his support. The ransom is of such a high amount that if I pay, I will fall under the control of my bank, which will have become the owner of my company. I will no longer have any autonomy."

An idea crossed Samantha; she told him:

"I heard that a competing company had sought to take over yours, a few months ago."

"That's right, but thanks to the loyalty of our shareholders, we escaped their takeover bid[5]."

Samantha had followed the adventures of the OPA as well as its failure in the media, she knew also that an investigation by the financial office of the FBI was in progress precisely regarding this company, she asked:

"Do you think that the company that tried to take control of yours could resort to less respectable ways to get your hands on your business?"

"You mean that..."

"This company may have links with the mafia that you don't know about, which would be normal since mafia networks do not operate in the open. I don't remember which bank was involved in the over?"

"It was BICM, the International Bank for World Commerce."

"So, this hypothesis must be ruled out, because an investigation is underway on the exorbitant remuneration of its leader, an American of Libyan origin. Now wouldn't be the time for them to act behind the scenes. That said, they can always try to persuade some of your shareholders to sell to gradually secure a majority. Have there been stock movements recently?"

"Yes, but not for a worrying amount. However, I learned that one of our oldest shareholders had dis-

---

5 Made to the shareholders of a company by another company seeking to take control of it.

posed of its shares. It surprised me, but the price was attractive, maybe he needs money."

"Have you contacted him?"

"No."

"I think it would be interesting to know the exact reasons that led to the sale of his titles. I could take care of this. What do you think Chris?"

"Um, it might scare them if they are the authors of this transaction, but why not? In any case, we must act. Stepping into the anthill might shed some light on the authors of the ransom demand and by extension, cause the release of Mrs. Smith, a lesser evil for them, rather than having a mega investigation into their covert activities."

Edward P. Smith exclaimed:

"So go ahead, go for it!"

"Chris, would you be, okay?"

"Yes, but I don't know. It's up to you and the FBI, not the job of police in our small town."

Samantha smiled; Chris hadn't grown in courage over time. She looked at the man he had become. He had put on weight; his chubby cheeks accentuated his childish air. For the first time in years, she felt outside the spider's web in which she was stuck in the old days. She felt an intense relief. She felt a renewed sense of freedom that left her thinking that she could finally start a new life.

7
CHICAGO, FBI OFFICE

As soon as she returned from Hinsdale, Samantha Gosvenor wrote an email to her superior, Romuald Brown, asking him for an urgent appointment. She told him that she had crucial information relating to the kidnapping of the wife of Edward P. Smith. To her great surprise, a few minutes later, she got an answer giving her an appointment for the next morning.

Romuald S. Brown was up early. He arrived at his office at seven o'clock. At eight o'clock sharp, Samantha knocked on his door which, however, was open.

"Hello Samantha, come in, settle down."

He pointed to the chair opposite his, she sat down and waited.

His head bent over his paper, he wrote manually, which gave Sam plenty of time to observe his incipient baldness. His short, already white hair curled. When he raised his head, he took off his little round glasses, folded them up and put them on the table. He closed his file, then finally, expressed himself:

"In your message, you do not tell me how you learned information about the drama of Princeton Road?"

Samantha explained it to him in a few words, he replied soberly:

"OK, anyway, we would have been seized of this matter sooner or later."

"Edward P. Smith asks that we remain discreet, and the press not be informed. He is afraid that the kidnappers will carry out their threat."

Romuald S. Brown smiled:

"As you're supposed to know, the FBI doesn't usually publicize the cases it's dealing with. Secrecy is at the heart of our actions."

Sam smiled back. She did not yet know her superior very well, but he seemed to conform to what she had heard. An intelligent man, endowed with humor and who knew how to make quick decisions. She waited for the continuation which came immediately:

"Since circumstances have decided so, you will lead this investigation. If you need help, I will put some at your disposal. From today, you can take with you an agent and a trainee. You will keep me informed, day by day, of the progress of your mission. Have you thought about your first step?"

"Well, I'm wondering if Mrs. Smith's kidnapping isn't related to the failure of the takeover bid on her husband's company. It was Edward P. Smith who put me on this track. One of its largest shareholders recently sold its stock package. I am going to ask to meet this man, it is important to know to whom these shares went."

"It's a good idea, given the stakes. Whatever you do, you must strictly apply the safety instructions in force. Each time you move, you will leave the place where you go with my assistant. You won't go anywhere unannounced, okay?"

"Yes sir."

"You didn't tell me the amount of the ransom, but it must be related to the Smith's wealth."

"I do not know it, E.P. Smith only indicated that the sum being very high, he was forced to meet his banker. He added that, because of the payment, his company would come under the control of his bank."

"That's what I thought, so I agree with you in assuming that the kidnapping may have a relationship with a company seeking to take control of Smithandco Investment. Going back to the beginning of this case, if I'm correctly informed, it's the delivery man of Pigeon Transport who discovered the body of the kidnappers' first victim?"

"Yes, but we are not certain that the attack on this woman is linked to the delivery."

"We can hypothesize that the coincidence between the two cases is not fortuitous. The decision-maker sends one of his henchmen to the Smiths' home, he thinks Mrs. Smith is in the house at the time. This individual, for some reason unknown to us, received the order to assassinate Mrs. Smith. He takes the woman who is present at his home to be her. All of this happens just before the delivery person arrives, as if the principal had wanted him to be accused. One can wonder if a snitch had not been placed on the truck of this poor guy. He was suspected of the assault, right?"

"Not exactly, Hinsdale Police Officer Christopher Flores suspected him of being an accomplice instead. He arrested him, then sent him to court to put pressure on him and make him confess his connection to the killer. His lawyer got him released on bail. It's the Pigeon Company Transport that paid, they don't need this kind of publicity."

"I can't help but think that the delivery man might be in cahoots with the killer... You must meet him urgently, even before seeing the shareholder. The role played by this delivery man seems to me the priority to clarify in this case. We must summon him here; will you know how to do it or should I ask a more experienced agent? Do you know how to use the polygraph[6]?"

Samantha hadn't considered her boss questioning her abilities when he had just put her in charge of the investigation, she replied very quickly:

"I know and I prefer to be alone in charge, at least initially."

"Okay, you report everything to me, in person."

"Very well, sir."

"Remember to go out armed, all the time, you're not dealing with altar boys, they almost killed outright, they can start over, if only to save time and to put more pressure on Smith to pay quickly."

"I always carry my small gun with me, the one I was given when I arrived here."

"Well, do you practice regularly in the shooting range?"

"Yes, sir, several times a week."

---

6 Also called the lie detector.

"Fine, I expect you tonight for a first debriefing."

"Tonight, already?"

"Yes, it's an ultra-sensitive matter. Sooner or later, I will have a call from my Ministry. If they don't know, they won't take long to know, if only through me who will be obliged to refer to the boss of the central, who himself will pass on to the Minister."

"Give me a little more time so that I have a first result."

Before answering, Romuald S. Brown fixed Agent Samantha Gosvenor with his piercing gaze, as if to assess her ability to cope. Instead of having very short hair like most of the female agents, Samantha had kept her long hair which she had swept back in a Strict doubly tied ponytail that totally exposed her pretty face and long, thin neck. Who knows if her beauty would not serve her in her mission? He decided to give her a delay before taking this business away from him which, a priori, he would have preferred to entrust to a better connoisseur of the environment, but it was perhaps only a postponement, because if afterwards, she revealed herself too slow or inefficient, he would not hesitate to replace her:

"I'll give you forty-eight hours, not an hour more."

"Very well, thank you sir."

Samantha got up and walked towards the door. Romuald S. Brown watched her leave his office. She turned around before crossing the threshold, noticed that he continued to follow her with his eyes, she bowed her head in his direction, then she went to her office, closed the door, grabbed her phone to call the delivery person's lawyer.

"Samantha Gosvenor, agent at the FBI office in Chicago. I have just been appointed as official investigator of the investigation into the disappearance of Mrs. Smith. I need to meet your client, Nick Kowalski, urgently. His testimony is essential to start my mission. Will you organize a meeting? Do not delay, otherwise I will summon him."

"I'll join him but spare him. He was very shaken by his arrest. Furthermore, he is currently not certain of being able to return to work soon."

"It's in his interest that I know more."

"OK, I will call him, let's say eleven o'clock at your office, shall we? I will assist him, that's sure."

"Fine, I'll expect you at eleven o'clock, unless otherwise modified by you."

Dr Rupert Kantorowicz rubbed his hands. As soon as the FBI entered the dance, it confirmed that this case would be a great springboard for his career. It was only too bad that, for the moment, not wanting to harm his client or alienate both the police of Hinsdale and the FBI office in Chicago, he could not communicate with the media, but his time would come, he was sure of it. For now, his priority was to call Nick. He got him right away. After having heard from little Alan, he informed him of the request of the FBI. Nick Kowalski had a reaction tinged with apprehension, he exclaimed:

"Rupert, are you sure I wouldn't be scared if I met that FBI agent?"

"No, on the contrary, it's in your interest, she's going to carry out an in-depth investigation with the means that the Hinsdale police don't have."

"She? Is she a woman, this agent?"

"Yes, her name is Samantha Gosvenor. She fixed the appointment at eleven o'clock today, at her FBI office in Chicago. I will assist you. A very positive point is that she knows the head of the Hinsdale Police. Let's meet there at ten fifty-five."

"Okay, I trust you."

Nick Kowalski hung up. He heard Sarah call him. He immediately joined her. Worried, frowning, she asked him:

"Who was calling you?"

"My lawyer, he asked me to find him at the FBI, to meet the agent who is assigned to the investigation."

"What is the FBI doing in your case? Would you be suspected, of what?"

"No, I do not think I am suspected; I am summoned as a witness. As there was a very serious attack and that Mrs. Smith has disappeared, it is normal that the FBI intervenes. The agent is a woman."

"A woman? Be careful, they are often tougher and more demanding than men."

"Sarah, how can you say such a thing?"

"Wherever they work, women are forced to do more than mem to be judged efficient and taken seriously. At the FBI, it must be like elsewhere, or even worse."

Nick remained silent. He checked his phone, it was nine-thirty. He would leave at ten to make sure to be on time. His grandmother was coming any minute. Sarah and the baby would not be alone, he rejoiced, for a muted fear had arisen in his mind since the discovery of the victim, which had been reinforced by his arrest. He sighed, went into the kitchenette to prepare a sandwich. He forced himself to eat it all, he wanted to have a full stomach before his interrogation.

At ten-fifty he walked into the FBI lobby. He waited until the arrival of his lawyer. Five minutes later, heading for the elevator, the lawyer clarified:

"The agent will ask you questions, I'll let you answer. I will record your statement, because for the moment, there is no question of an interrogation. If a question disturbs you, you tell me, and I will speak. Agreed?"

"Yes, thanks."

At eleven o'clock sharp, they were at the door of Samantha Gosvenor's office. She didn't lose any time, she greeted them, asked them to sit down and immediately broached the matter:

"Hello, Mr. Kowalski. Let's get started, shall we?"

"Hello Madam, I'm listening."

"I read your testimony to the Hinsdale police officer, I'm not going to make you repeat it, I'm just going to ask you a few questions about the events. Before arriving at the client's, Mr. Kowalski, did you call to make sure there would be someone in the house?"

"Yes, as usual, I called from the previous stop. A woman answered me."

"How long did it take between your call and your arrival at the Smiths' home?"

"It's hard to say precisely because I had trouble finding the entrance to the Smiths' house. A very dense hedge of shrubs hides the access."

"If you don't remember, as you are being tracked from the central post of your company, can you specifically ask them the following question: At which time precisely did you effect the delivery preceding that of Mr. Smith?"

"I…"

Faced with the emotion of Nick Kowalski, the lawyer spoke:

"Listen, I'm going to take care of it. I'll do it right away, if you think it's an important information."

"Yeah, timing is everything in this case. We also know that Mrs. Smith asked for a nanny at noon sharp."

Rupert immediately called Pigeon Transport, he introduced himself as Nick Kowalski's lawyer, he asked for the delivery schedule department. They transferred him, he asked his question to the interlocutor who made him wait a few moments, time for him to consult the schedule for the given day. A rapper's music popped in his ear, he put his phone away… Pigeon Transport had very bad taste… As soon as his interlocutor resumed the call, he clicked on the top speaker so that Samantha Gosvenor could hear the answer at the same time as him:

"Good, I took Nick Kowalski's file. The delivery that preceded that of Mr. Smith took place at eleven fifty. Nick Kowalski arrived at 12:30 at Mr. Smith."

The lawyer thanked him, asked that a photocopy of Nick Kowalski's detailed schedule be sent to his firm, then he hung up. Samantha Gosvenor addressed Nick Kowalski:

"Mr. Kowalski, your client, Mrs. Smith didn't call Nurse Services until noon. So, she was the one who answered you ten minutes earlier. This implies that she decided to call for a babysitter suddenly. I think Christopher Flores asked for her list of calls."

The lawyer intervened:

"Yes, he did, and he undertook to communicate it to me."

"Mrs. Smith may have received a call for an unscheduled meeting, which would have forced her to use *Nurses Services*. The more we manage to specify the sequence of acts of all the protagonists, the more we can specify the role of the aggressor. I have no other questions to ask yourself right now. You'll sign your statement, and you can leave."

Rupert Kantorowicz was not surprised. She was starting her investigation; she didn't yet have the information that he himself had gathered.

As he walked back to the elevator, he couldn't help thinking that if he had met the young woman in other circumstances, he would have offered her dinner somewhere... apart from her strict hairstyle, she was really something.

As he and Nick walked back to the FBI lobby, he turned back to Nick and said:

"Well then, it was not too painful, was it?"

"No, I was very scared, but finally, it went well, thanks to you, baby."

Nick bit his lip, the nickname he had once given to Rupert had escaped him. He blushed, tried to recover:

"Excuse me, Rupert, I…"

"Don't worry, you're excused, it doesn't matter if you don't use this qualifier in front of a witness. Come on, go home and kiss baby Alan for me."

Nick left, grateful. Fortunately, he was not alone in this horrible story. He rejoiced that Rupert had agreed to defend him. Without him, he didn't know if he would have held the shock.

8

Back to deliveries, sooner than expected.

Nick was having a lovely late afternoon with Sarah. His grandmother had left quite early for his uncle's. They were quiet, Alan was sound asleep. Sarah was beginning to be less tired. The stove was humming and throwing up beautiful flames. It was a superb spectacle. Sarah was embroidering a cushion and watching television while Nick leafed through a cooking magazine. He loved cooking, he was constantly looking for new recipes that he could try. He stopped short at the photograph of a custard tart which made his mouth water. He marked the page by folding its corner, he would prepare it one day or another. It was both simple and tasty. At six o'clock, his phone vibrated. He took it out of his pocket. Ann Pham's number, his manager at the warehouse, was displayed.

"Good evening, Nick, I hope all is well for you. I need you to come and give us a helping hand, tomorrow morning."

Nick was flabbergasted. It wasn't that he didn't want to work again, but really, Pigeon Transport had granted him a month's paid leave. And now, he was being asked to come back to work the next day! He said:

"I thought I had a month's paid leave."

"Sorry, Nick, I have no choice. Several of your colleagues have caught COVID, they are unavailable. I'm counting on you tomorrow at seven-thirty."

Nick didn't have time to look for another argument, Ann Pham had hung up. Half an hour later, he was still holding his phone. Meanwhile, Sarah had fallen asleep on her chair. He felt the rigidity of his right hand which had remained clenched on his phone, as if it were glued to it. His amazement had been so great.

Nick hadn't even been able to ask if he had the right to keep the month pay. What should he do? He knew that if he didn't show up at the warehouse, he would run the risk of losing his job altogether. The worse was telling Sarah about his return to work. Contrary to what he expected, she accepted the change calmly and without protest. She even added, smiling:

"In fact, it may be preferable. Here, you find it difficult to occupy yourself and imagine, with the month extra pay, the three of us could go on vacation."

Sarah's reaction comforted him.

They went to bed early. At four o'clock in the morning, Alan made himself heard. Nick woke up and watched Sarah grab the little one and put him to her breast, then, when he was full, put him back in his basket. She immediately went to sleep. He gazed at her for a long time, gently caressed her back, then he tried to sleep, but without success. He ended up going downstairs, made himself some coffee, cursing the din of the machine. During the day, from his truck, he would call the after-sales service, because the decibels of the product far exceeded those announced in the technical description. He went to a consumer forum and saw that he was not the only user of the same device to complain about its noise and lack of stability. He added his testimony.

After swallowing a double coffee, he took a shower by running a trickle of lukewarm water, then he examined his beard in the mirror, it was still tolerable. On his next day off, he would drop by the barber's shop to have it trimmed. He looked at his watch, six o'clock, it was a little early to leave, but he wasn't going to sit there doing nothing, he went out. A mist prevented him from seeing far, he headed for the parking lot where he parked his car. Len, the guard, was dozing, he opened the eyes as he came along:

"Hi Nick! How are you? Back to work already?"

"No choice, they called me back yesterday, they asked me to start again this morning. Seems that they are short of delivery people."

"Oh boy, these bastards! I hope they won't take the opportunity to ask you to reimburse your leave, they would be quite capable of it."

"Yeah, but deep down, I wonder if it won't be better for me to work than to go around in circles at my house."

"I hope for you that everything will work out, that they will arrest the killer of this poor girl. It's not fair that it fell on her."

"You forget the woman who was kidnapped."

"Do you believe in that? Wouldn't she be an accomplice? With what I saw on TV, I find this whole situation weird, don't you?"

"It's complicated, I leave that to the investigators. I am just a little delivery man who found himself caught in this trap."

"Yeah, I pity you, but now everyone has heard of you. Who knows if Netflix or another platform will ever call you to shoot a fiction with what happened to you?"

"I wish it had never happened to me, as for participating in a series, no, I refuse!"

Len said nothing more, he watched Nick go to his car, come back, swipe his card to get out of the car park. He waved his hand at him, then fell back into a half-sleep, he couldn't wait for his night shift to end. Then he would continue with his student day at the Northwestern University.

Nick took the direction of the warehouse; he had a twenty minutes' drive. At this early hour, traffic was smooth. He arrived early, his supervisor was not there, he fell on the dispatcher who had been on night duty.

"Hi, Nick Kowalski, I resume today, Ann called me yesterday."

"Ah, I am not aware. She hasn't arrived, I'm finishing the night's deliveries."

"I can't start loading?"

"No, she is the one who organizes the schedule of delivery men who will leave later. We have a hell of a recruiting problem right now."

"I am in a good position to know, I was not supposed to work this month, I was on leave."

"You had a month's leave? Incredible, man, I didn't know that existed at our place! Hey, speaking of the devil, here she comes."

Nick waited until Ann Pham got out of her car and she walked to her office. Well, it was a cubicle rather than an office, because she worked in a windowless room that overlooked the hallway that led to the warehouse room.

He saw her put down her bag, take off her jacket and put on a sweater, he walked towards her:

"Hello Ann, here I am."

"Okay, Nick, hello. Take truck 1, you can load it. I changed your route because I thought you wouldn't appreciate taking the same one after what happened. Here is your roadmap."

"Thank you, that's nice."

"Have a good day."

"Thanks. I am going."

Nick looked at the column of trucks waiting to be loaded. His was first, its mouth open. He considered the parcels piled up on the carts, checked that they were indeed prepared to be delivered north of Chicago. This was the case. As he was early, he had time to combine its successive deliveries intelligently. He turned on his phone's GPS, indicated the towns to serve, then he compared the route obtained with his route map. Then, he started loading the packages to be delivered last. The more he loaded, the closer he got to his first stops. The worst that could arrive during the day, was having to clear packages to get hold of the one he had to deliver, even though he had arrived at the delivery point. There was a great risk, then, to get the wrong package and customer.

Loading took him an hour. After that he could leave. He did not know the north route, but he had noticed that his stops were quite close to one another. To begin with, in accordance with his choice of loading, he chose to go directly to the most distant destination and make deliveries on the return route. Gradually, on the road to Desplaines, Nick relaxed. Certainly, it was not the path he should have followed if he had respected his roadmap, but driving made him feel good, especially driving without marking a stop. The 33 kilometers went too quickly.

He ended up in front of the Mac Donald Museum, where he took a selfie for Alan later, then he crossed to reach the Mac Do on the other side of the road, which was in business. He drank a coffee and ate a bacon, egg and cheese mac-muffin.

This time, he felt full, he got back into his truck, started his deliveries. Five in Desplaines itself, that went off without a hitch. He then took the road to Northbrook. For a good while, he was busy in the district of the old city of Techny, with many stops. It made you think that Northbrook was devoid of convenience stores. Among the packages, he brought a washing machine that the customer forced him to unpack to check that it was indeed the machine which he had ordered. Although this service was not part of his obligations, Nick agreed to carry it to his laundry room. He didn't even have the satisfaction of a good tip. Yet, the customer lived in a beautiful house with a beautiful garden. He understood the reason when leaving, there was a sign on which the name of the client and his profession were inscribed: Landscaper. He dreamed for a moment, Northbrook was a beautiful place, it could be one of the towns where he would have liked to live if he had exercised a lucrative profession... He sighed. It wasn't tomorrow that he would have the means to live in this kind of place... But Alan, yes, he would! Invigorated by the thought of the future life of his child, Nick completed his deliveries ahead of schedule. He drove back to the warehouse. It was four o'clock when he reported his day to Ann Pham. She congratulated him on his speed:

"Well done! You were quick. You can take charge of half a truck, we we're in a rush."

Nick paled, he had expected to go home earlier, he felt tired. He tried to refuse:

"I had planned to go home. Because of the little one, I don't sleep much. Besides, I arrived early this morning, I started before the scheduled time."

"All the more reason to accept. I'll score you four more hours; don't you need money? Children are expensive. For my part, I started putting money aside as soon as my daughter was born, to pay for her higher education. I opened an account for her on purpose, you should do the same. If you do, Pigeon Transport adds its share. Do you know? The boss said he wanted his employees to benefit from the possibility of building up a pension, but I don't care for the pension. On the other hand, if my daughter has a well-paid job later, she will help me. This is what retirement is in my country of origin, the children pay for their parents, they reimburse them for what they have done for them in their youth."

"Oh no, I don't want my little Alan to pay for me when I'm old, I want him to enjoy what he will make. I really want him to have the good life that I do not have. Alright, come on, what route did you put me on this time?"

"On the usual one. I authorize you to return the truck only tomorrow morning when you will take your shift, is that okay?"

"I do not know; it will force me to plan for my parking. A truck is bigger than my car."

"Ah well, especially yours. What an idea to have such a small car!"

Nick ignored what he considered a criticism. Yes, he was content with his little Ford, it only cost him a hundred dollars a month, while some of his colleagues left a good part of their pay in monthly payments for luxury vehicles... He himself would never have a Rolls or a Jaguar, but Alan would have one, one that he would not pay by monthly payments too high compared to his salary!

While he would have preferred to return home, Nick made the best of it, he took the additional route. He was returning against his will, very close to the scene of the tragedy. He had goosebumps as he passed just off the Princeton Road. He came to mutter: *I believe that I would not have managed to deliver in this cursed street!*

Very strangely, a few moments later, he was seized by an impulse, so strong that he yielded to it, he found himself, when he had only one more stop to make, in front of the house of the drama. He got out of the truck, went to the residence. It was plunged into silence and darkness. No exterior lights turned on. He approached the door, knocked without worrying about the cameras. No one answered his call. The house was no longer inhabited. He stomped back to his truck. He took the road to his last stop, then he returned home, immersed in what had happened, only two weeks earlier...

9

A STRANGE MEETING

Samantha Gosvenor read the email she had received that morning for the third time:

Good morning! I learned that you have been put in charge of the investigation into the Princeton Road attack and the kidnapping of Natasha Smith. I have information to send you, but I don't want to take the risk of signing my true name. If you want to know more, you can call me at the following number on which I have a subscription which will end in two hours.

A phone number followed.

Samantha Gosvenor started to think. She had no choice, she had to reach the author of the message, even if he was a prankster. Before typing the number, she went to the service specializing in surveillance of telephones, she found the person nicknamed Space X, because he claimed that his first name, Adolf, was impossible and had exposed him to sneers and incessant teasing throughout his schooling.

"Hi Space, here is the number at which I am to reach a stranger, could you locate the device?"

"Yeah, no problem, I give you my word, but once your call is located, what will you do?"

"I don't know."

"I advise you to be assisted by at least two agents who would help you get your hands on your dude if that's what you have in mind."

"You're right, but I have not yet formed my team and do I have time? He gave me two hours and half an hour has already gone."

"Well, hurry up. In the meantime, I can try to find out what operator is behind this number."

"Okay, see you soon."

Samantha Gosvenor immediately went to the agent assignment department where Grace Ivory ruled, a middle-aged woman of imposing build who always dressed in pink.

"Hi Grace, this is an absolute urgency. I am in charge of an investigation and the boss authorized me to be assisted by two people, an agent and a trainee."

"OK Sam, I'll see who is available right away."

Grace Ivory immersed herself in her files, then she raised her head and, smiling, she announced:

"Agent Michael Spring and a trainee, Amina Goma, a small one who is with us for two weeks and that's good, she dreams of participating in a criminal investigation. She has confided that this was the reason for her stay here, she is a psychology student and is preparing her research dissertation in criminology."

"Perfect, can you send them to my office? I have a mission for them at once."

"I'll see. I hope Spring is there, as for Amina, she came this morning to ask whether I had anything for her, she'll be enthusiastic. She'll be in your office in a few minutes."

"I prefer that you send me Spring at the same time as her, it is he who will pilot her. Thanks Grace, see you later."

"See you later, Samantha."

Grace Ivory reached Michael Spring:

"Hi Mike, I have a job for you. Samantha Gosvenor asked for two people for an immediate mission, I told her that you were available, she is waiting for you in her office."

"Gosvenor... I don't know her well, she arrived recently. Does the order come from the boss?"

"Yes, of course, you will be assisted by Amina Goma, the trainee."

"All right, I'm coming."

Michael Spring grabbed his jacket, he made sure his service weapon was in his belt holster. He then went to the office occupied by Samantha Gosvenor. It was odd to find himself at the door of the office which was previously that of one of his best buddies, who had been murdered three months earlier... Did Samantha Gosvenor know?

He knocked and entered without waiting for an answer.

"Michael Spring, hello Samantha. Seems you need backup?"

"Yes, please sit down. I'm in charge of the Smith case investigation."

Impressed, Mickael Spring could not help whistling, then he said:

"Oh, not bad!"

"In this context, I need to send you to a place which that for the moment I ignore. Let me explain, I received a message from a stranger who claims to have information on the Smith case. I'll call him as soon as we can locate the call. You will be assisted by a trainee, Amina Goma. You will have to go to the place of the call the soonest possible, I will try to make the exchange last as long as I can by making the interlocutor speak."

"Can I see the message?"

"Yes, of course, I printed it, here it is."

"Hmm, the message is clear, he asks you to call, and the goal is to set an appointment. That will really surprise me if we have time to get there, he will be gone."

"I have no choice, we must try."

"OK, but you must inform us as soon as you know the address of the meeting, which will allow us to reach you on site."

"Yes of course."

Someone knocked at the door. It was Amina Goma:

"Hello Agent Gosvenor, did you ask me to come?"

"Yes, hello Amina, sit down. You will assist Michael Spring here. Now that you are both here, I will call my correspondent, I put the loudspeaker."

Samantha dialed the stranger's number:

"Hello, Samantha Gosvenor, FBI agent, I'm listening."

"Hello Samantha, glad you accept. I'm waiting for you at the office of the car rental agency, SIXT,

714 S Wabash Ave. It takes 10 minutes to get there, I allow you a margin of 10 minutes, it will give you time to collect your car and park on site."

The caller hung up immediately. Samantha Gosvenor called Space X:

"Do you have anything?"

"The subway station, Grand Central, blinked, he's over there."

"OK, since it works, continue to follow him, you would tell me then if he made other calls and where he's calling from. As soon as his subscription ends, you will relay with my phone. Thanks!"

She hung up, then addressed her acolytes:

"OK, let's go. I will let you go a little before the meeting point, you will join me there when I press your contact. Here is my duplicate car key."

"OK."

They rushed to the parking lot and Samantha raced towards the meeting place. Eleven minutes later, her two acolytes left the car a hundred meters before the SIXT agency.

She herself parked in the parking lot of the car rental company, then she showed up at the agency. There were clients in the waiting room, she sat down in an armchair and texted her informant. He replied immediately:

"I saw you. Get out of the office, my rental car is parked right out front, it's open, come, I'll join you there."

Samantha bit her lip. It didn't go as planned, she clicked on the contact with Michael: *He takes me in his car, follow us. My car is parked in the SIXT car park, hurry up!*

She took as long as possible to get out of the agency, then she got into the rental car, a bright red Beetle... Next to her, behind the wheel, was a young-looking man, wearing a wig. Its red hair was abnormally shiny... He had dark glasses that concealed the color of his eyes.

He drove off immediately, gliding with astonishing ease through the heavy traffic. He left downtown Chicago, took the north route. Twenty minutes later he stopped the car in front of a building under construction. He invited his passenger to get off:

"Here we are."

He freed the metal barrier that shut off access to the site, entered the house without windows, followed by Samantha. He pulled out a miniature flashlight. They entered a room sparsely furnished overlooking the back of the house. The windows were covered with wooden panels and a hurricane lamp sat in the middle of the room. The man sat down on one of the two canvas armchairs facing each other. Samantha did the same. She waited for him to speak:

"Let's get to what I must tell you. I am a private detective. I was hired by Mrs. Natacha Stoica-Smith to prepare for her divorce."

Samantha bit back a remark.

"I haven't gathered the evidence yet, but I suspect Edward P. Smith was behind the abduction of his wife."

"Why would he have done that?"

"I think he found out his wife wanted a divorce, and he cannot stand it."

"How did you get this idea?"

"I noticed Mrs. Smith was being followed. The day she disappeared, she called me before leaving home to let me know that her schedule had changed. She had a meeting with one of her friends at the Botanic Garden café. It was impossible for me to free myself in such a short time. We agreed that we would take stock in the evening. She didn't call me as expected, I got worried. As she had left me the coordinates of her friend, I was able to reach her, I met her that same evening. Her name is Dorothy Flowers, she told me that she had not joined Natacha that day and even less given an appointment. Here is her phone number, she could tell you more about Natacha Stoica Smith."

"Thank you for the clarification. Now I would like to understand why you contacted me."

"I don't have the means to find Mrs. Stoica-Smith. Besides, I don't have a mandate to do it. But you, you have them. When I learned that the FBI was involved, I immediately thought that I should reach the agent in charge of the investigation. I inquired, I learned that it was you."

"And why did you take all these precautions before speaking to me?"

"As I told you, I suspect Mr. Smith of the abduction of his wife. I'm nobody in front of him... If he wants to kill me, he pays a killer and I disappear. The investigation would be short, I am an independent private investigator, it would quickly conclude that one of my customers or opponents wanted revenge. I want to live, that's all."

"How long have you worked for Mrs. Smith?"

"Four months. She contacted me through a friend, Gregory Trousers for whom I had previously worked. I'll give you his contact details if needed, but I don't want to establish any official contact with you."

"Okay, thanks for the information. If afterwards, I need to contact you again, how can I do it?"

"I'll call you from time to time to get news of the investigation. Come on, we must go. I don't need to take you back, we were followed by your collaborators, I imagine that you will return with them."

Samantha opened her mouth, she was surprised by the stranger's insight, but she didn't answer.

Discreetly, she clicked on her watch to take a picture. She would ask if the identification service could put a name on this individual.

He got into his car. Samantha warned her partners that she was waiting for them. They arrived two minutes later. She told them most of what she had just learned. Michael Spring objected:

"If he didn't tell you his name, know that I managed to take a picture of him with my zoom."

Samantha, instead of saying that she too had been able to photograph him, congratulated him. She guessed that Michael Spring, older than her in the house, had a hard time putting up with being led by her, who was younger and moreover female... So, she had to leave him some leeway to favor their relationship in the interest of the investigation. They returned to the office. Samantha asked Michael Spring to take care of the detective's identification, then she informed him that she herself was going to reach the shareholder of Smithandco Investment, the financial company run by PE Smith. Previously, she closeted herself in her office, consulted the list of addresses she had collected since her arrival. Having found the contact she was looking for, she clicked on Denys Dupont who worked at the regional office of the SEC[7]. She reached him without difficulty, went straight to the point:

"Hello Denys, Samantha Gosvenor, FBI office in Chicago. I took over from Gaby Dor with whom you were in contact. Would you be available for us to meet urgently?"

"Hello, yes, I actually had the opportunity to exchange information with Gaby. To what do I owe the pleasure of your proposal?"

"I would prefer to talk to you about it in person. It's noon, we could take advantage of it and have lunch together?"

"Why not? I haven't planned anything for lunch. Who takes care of the meal, you, or me?"

"I can go to the Italian, where can we meet?"

"The weather is nice and not too cold, what do you think of Millennium Park? Let us meet at the Cloud Gate[8]. Then, we will find a free bench."

"Fine, see you later."

Samantha Gosvenor would have preferred the meeting to be within walking distance, but it was normal to let her correspondent choose the place since she was the requester. Before going down to the parking lot, she stopped at the Italian and chose the

---

7 The US Securities and Exchange Commission, commonly referred to as the Securities and Exchange Commission, often abbreviated as the SEC, is the US federal agency for regulating and supervising the financial markets.
8 *Gate of the clouds, also called Bean.* Sculpture created by Anish Kapoor in 2006 in Millennium Park in Chicago.

menu of the day, pasta with tomatoes and salmon and for dessert, a peach tiramisu. She added two beers, then went to get her car.

Fifteen minutes later, she parked close to Millennium Park. She headed towards the Cloud Gate. She was not alone, many passers-by took selfies in the middle of gigantic mirrors. She sent an SMS to Denys Dupont to warn him of her arrival. Instead of answering her, he appeared at her side, apostrophized her in a low voice:

"So, FBI agent, is that how you protect yourself?"

Smiling, Samantha replied to him back and forth:

"I could tell you the same, SEC agent!"

"Let's go, I do not have much time for you."

"OK."

They moved quickly towards the museum. A little further on, they settled on an isolated bench. Samantha took out the boxes that contained their meal. She gave his share to Denys Dupont. After having started her beer, she attacked the subject of their meeting:

"I am currently conducting an investigation in which Edward P. Smith appears. I have learned that one of the shareholders of his investment company had recently sold his portfolio. What do you know about this?"

"To tell you the truth, relations are quite tense between Smith and the SEC. These last years, Smithandco Investment was condemned to pay several penalties for irregular operations, even suspicious ones. Recently, the company was the target of a takeover bid launched by a Chinese financier group. This takeover failed. It is true that one of its major shareholders sold his actions and this operation alerted us. However, after verification, the buyers are diverse, they have no connection between them. Yet they have one thing in common, they are all Japanese investors."

"Well, I'll tell you what's happening on my side. I ask you to keep the secret. Mrs. Smith has been kidnapped. Smith reports a ransom demand from her sequestrators whose amount is so high that his company would become the property of his creditors if he paid it. I wonder if the kidnapping of his wife would not be linked to the failed OPA."

"In other words, you are asking me to provide you with information on the purchasers of the sold shares?"

"Yes, that would be a first step. You could give me their identities, we have the means then to launch investigations to try to see if these investors may have a link with the Chinese group, initiator of the take-over bid."

"On this point, I can answer you right away. There are three Japanese investors, who work regularly with China. Smithandco cannot claim not to having been a party to this exchange of shares, because the company has a major subsidiary which operates on the Japanese market and which it uses for its transactions with China."

"Why would Smith let it happen?"

"He hasn't done very well in recent months. He grew considerably richer during the first year of the pandemic, doubling his profit, but since the recovery, business is not so good, the share price was immediately affected. The OPA intervened when the stock started to fall. It failed because the offered price was too low, the shareholders preferred to wait."

"Except the one who sold?"

"He sold when the buy-in period set for the take-over bid had elapsed, and the share price had gone up again. Many exchanges have taken place, we are monitoring them. So far, nothing out of the ordinary has been reported since the sale. With regard to the kidnapping of Mrs. Smith, do you have a lead?"

"I can't help thinking it is connected in some way to Smith's society."

"Do you think that those who wanted to appropriate the company would have resorted to this villainous means to succeed where the OPA failed?"

"Yes, but I do not exclude that Smith plays an active part in the case."

"In other words, do you suspect him of being an accomplice in the kidnapping of his wife?"

"Absolutely, I learned that she wanted a divorce, and he did not agree."

Denys Dupont remained a long moment without speaking. Did Samantha Gosvenor speak seriously? He could not give any credibility to the words of the replacement for Gaby Dor. Really, was a boss capable of endangering his business for vulgar problems in a marriage? It was only possible if this woman had the means to exert influence. However, to his knowledge, Natacha Stoica-Smith did not own any shares in her husband's company. However, an idea occurred to him:

"Mrs. Smith is of Romanian origin, could she have a connection with the Romanian environment in the United States?"

"Nothing is impossible, I thought about it. That would be another lead, but I'll explore first Smith's. Well, thank you for this exchange, I am delighted to have made your acquaintance. Call me in the case of new information, do we agree?"

Denys Dupont was surprised by Samantha's bluntness, she hadn't even finished her meal, they had only exchanged a few words and she already wanted to leave? However, he did not insist to prolong their meeting, she was certainly stressed by her investigation. He recognized that having Edward P. Smith in your sights was anything but simple. He was a very powerful man... Denys Dupont just replied:

"Yes, it's okay."

Denys Dupont watched Samantha Gosvenor get up. She had a slender and sinewy figure. Admittedly, he couldn't admire her legs because of her outfit, but he could imagine them thanks to her ankles which were uncovered. He smiled, he hadn't lost in the exchange, the replacement for Gaby Dor was a real good surprise. Not only did she seem competent, but in addition, she was very attractive...

10
Hinsdale Hospital

Christopher Flores had just been notified that Rosa Williams, the woman who was seriously injured at Edward P. Smith's home, could be questioned. He called Samantha Gosvenor.

"Hi Sam, I have good news for you! The doctor who follows the Smith's nanny at the hospital has just given permission to interview her."

"Oh, that's great news! Thanks, Chris for letting me know."

"I guess you'll rush, I would like to be present at your interrogation, would you accept?"

Samantha Gosvenor was surprised that Christopher was making this request since the investigation had been taken away from him. Furthermore, for personal reasons, she wanted to keep him at a distance, so she didn't answer immediately, then she said quite abruptly:

"The investigation is in the hands of the FBI, in what capacity would you come?"

"I promise not to intervene and let you lead the exchange, but it would interest me to be there. This case intrigues me."

"I don't know if your presence would be appropriate. Given the patient's condition, I assume that the interrogation will take place in the hospital room?"

"Yes."

"The two of us would be cramped. Besides, maybe she would speak more easily if I were alone and because I am a woman."

"Yes, but as soon as she finds out you work for the FBI, she'll be scared."

"Not at all, everyone knows that crimes are the responsibility of the FBI."

"Besides, you'll have to tell her about Natacha Smith's kidnapping."

"Do you seriously think she does not know?"

"She was in no condition to follow the news."

Samantha recognized that Chris had arguments to justify his coming, so she gave in:

"Okay."

"Are you meeting me at Hinsdale Hospital or picking me up from the police station?"

"I'll join you there. Be careful, you don't get in touch with her before I arrive, we agree, and you will be there as a mere spectator?"

"Yes, I'll make myself very small."

"OK, see you soon".

Samantha had mixed feelings, she was delighted to meet the nurse but at the same time, she couldn't explain Christopher's request. Why did he want to attend the interrogation? Well, she didn't have time to seriously consider this question. The main thing was that she could collect the testimony of the victim. She went down to the parking lot to pick up her car and drove to Hinsdale Adventist Hospital where she arrived three quarters of an hour later. Christopher was waiting for her in the hall, he rushed to her as soon as she appeared.

"Hi Sam, I inquired, she is in room 314, on the third floor."

"OK."

Outside the door of room 314, a man stood guard. Christopher greeted him:

"Hello, Christopher Flores, from Hinsdale Police Station and this is Samantha Gosvenor from the FBI, we are authorized to interview Rosa Williams."

"Hello, I know, can you show me your cards?"

Sam and Chris complied.

"It's okay, I would like to point out that the doctor recommends not to exceed a period of 20 minutes, Mrs. Williams is very weak."

"We understand, see you later."

Samantha entered, followed by Christopher. She walked over to the young woman's bed.

"Hello Mrs. Williams, I'm Samantha Gosvenor from the FBI, I am in charge of the investigation on the Smith case. I'm going to ask you a few questions about the assault you suffered in home of the Smiths."

Rosa Williams looked at her with her large, dark, sunken eyes. Her hair was profuse and curly, her features drawn, she was pale under her brown skin. She sat up, leaned her head on her pillows and with this movement, she winced in pain. She closed her eyes for a minute, then she said:

"Hello, I'm listening."

"Thanks for your help. The day you came to the Smiths to babysit their child, what were the circumstances?"

"I was notified at the last minute; the agency called me a little after noon asking if I could go to the Smiths' house immediately."

"Had you ever been to the Smiths?"

"Yes, several times. I live nearby, the agency knows it and calls me first."

"So, you know Mrs. Smith?"

"Not really, but she trusts me, because the agency only employs qualified nurses. Also, when I got to her house, she gave me her instructions and left immediately."

"Tell me exactly how your arrival went that day."

"Mrs. Smith was in a great hurry, even more than the other times. She barely said *hello* to me, and she left. I remember her words: *Hello Rosa, do as usual, I'm in a hurry, we will see each other presently.* She didn't even tell me what time she would be back. I put my things down, and I went to see little Edward junior, he was asleep, I went downstairs to prepare his meal. That's when I was assaulted, passed out, and woke up in the hospital."

"In your opinion, how much time elapsed between your arrival and the attack?"

"A few minutes."

"Do you remember the individual who attacked you?"

"He was like a shadow. Very tall, he was at least a head taller than me and I'm not small. He was dressed entirely in black; he wore a mask and dark glasses."

"What happened?"

"It went very quickly, I remember the pain from his first stab wound, I immediately lost consciousness."

"Have you smelled a particular smell?"

"No, apart from a smell of hashish, but it's so common that it's rather the absence of the smell which could have been a distinctive sign."

"He smelled strong?"

"Yes, very strong. It permeates the clothes, the hair, suddenly, I don't know why, I told myself that he hadn't washed his hair, that was my last thought before I lost consciousness."

"Do you remember his voice?"

"It's difficult, he just said: *Hello Mrs. Smith! Ah, no one told me you were a woman of color!* He had a metallic, cold voice, the voice of a killer. He came to kill. I do not understand how I can be alive."

"It is possible that the arrival of the delivery man scared off your assailant. You probably owe him your life."

"It's incredible, I did not know that a delivery was planned. It's weird that Mrs. Smith didn't tell me, she must have forgotten."

"I agree with you, especially since he delivered a washing machine."

"Tell me, I heard over the radio that Mrs. Smith had been kidnapped."

Samantha hesitated, should she give her more information? Then she decided:

"Indeed, and his kidnappers have come forward."

"I think the killer took me for Mrs. Smith. They wanted to kill her, why then kidnap her instead of murdering her?"

"For the moment, the situation is far from clear. Luckily, you remember the words of your attacker about your skin color, this confirms that he had come for the purpose of assassinating Mrs. Smith."

Rosa Williams frowned, suddenly very preoccupied, she asked:

"The little one, what has become of him? He didn't attack him too?"

"No, don't worry, your attacker didn't go upstairs, probably for lack of time because of the arrival of the delivery man."

"So much the better, this child is cute and it's not his fault if he is the child of such parents."

"What do you mean?"

"He has a weird mother and an absent father. Yet they have everything, these people! Mr. and Mrs. Smith are very wealthy, their home is a palace. They have everything one can dream of. In the basement there is a projection room. In all the rooms, there are the trendiest gadgets. If you saw their kitchen! It's incredible, all the devices are controlled by voice. The fridge opens and pulls out what you ask for. For example, if I say: The kid's lunch", the corresponding box is brought out by a tube which opens and once the box is placed on the table, the tube retracts and stores itself. Then the box gets automatically in the oven, the dish is heated at the right temperature and all I have to do is feed the little one."

The door opened at that moment; the authoritative voice of a doctor was heard:

"Hello, the time I granted you is over, please leave my patient to rest."

Samantha turned around, a small man had entered, he was wearing a white blouse and looked stern. Samantha replied:

"Hello doctor, thank you for allowing us access to Mrs. Williams."

She turned to Rosa Williams and thanked her:

"Thank you very much for your testimony. I wish you to return home soon."

"Thank you, Madam, I hope that on your side, you will succeed in finding my attacker and deliver Mrs. Smith."

"Your version of the facts should help us. Bye, Madam."

Samantha left the room, followed by Christopher Flores who remained silent until the hospital car park. As Samantha walked to her car, Christopher suggested:

"Would you be free for lunch? Besides, if you could drive me, I'd be fine, I'm came on foot, from the station."

"Why not? We will take the opportunity to exchange our points of view on the testimony of this woman."

"Could we go to Il poggiolo? It is still early; it would be quiet there."

"Good idea, I love Italian food when it's good. You wouldn't recommend me a restaurant if it was not excellent. Tell me the way, you will be a better guide than my GPS."

Ten minutes later, they settled down in the restaurant dining room.

Christopher began the discussion:

"So, what's your opinion?"

"I need to think. I recorded the interview, I want to take the time to listen to it, I would like to assess the tone of her voice. I get the impression that she told her story as if she had not experienced it herself, as if another woman had been assaulted."

"Curious, this idea did not occur to me. To me, this man had come to kill Mrs. Smith on behalf of a third party, he carries his order but takes Rosa Williams for Mrs. Smith. He cannot accomplish his task because of the arrival of the delivery man."

"The killer certainly tells his sponsor that his contract is fulfilled, and same time, he probably mentions the skin color of the victim."

"I agree with you. It follows that Mrs. Smith is abducted, but if it is at her home, that would mean she hadn't left. Well, for the moment, I prefer that we leave it there, I'm hungry, the smell of pizzas makes my mouth water."

"OK, you're right, the pizzas are very tasty, thick, soft, garnished as nowhere else. When I eat here, to limit the damage, I choose the vegetarian."

"As long as I am taking a pizza, I'll go all out and order one with four cheeses."

Christopher hailed a waiter to order.

"Tell me, Chris, how's Hinsdale Police Station?"

"It's quiet, the city is generally quiet. Of course, there are young people who get drunk and take drugs, but as people have money, many are medically treated, which limits the disasters. That said, from time to time there is still a teenager who dies of an overdose."

"Creepy! I wouldn't like to be the parent of one of these crazy kids."

"There are a thousand ways to get damaged, sport extreme, motorcycling without a helmet, playing with weapons... As the external danger has largely disappeared - at least in our country - life no longer appears as dangerous, while the lifespan has never been so long. Young people reinvent danger, they play with death. Sometimes death wins."

"What do you mean, life is no longer dangerous?"

"Diseases are overcome sooner or later. Sometimes I wonder if human beings don't have the need to experience danger, even come close to death to regain a taste for life."

Samantha Gosvenor didn't comment on Christopher's last sentence. She herself had always loved life so much. It is true that since she had been a secret agent, she had experienced the danger of death. In those moments, the adrenaline rose so violently that when she got out of trouble, she inhaled deeply the pleasure of living.

She devoured her huge pizza with appetite, while telling herself that she would not be able to finish it, except that twenty minutes later, only small bits of dough remained on the plate. She drank a coffee to try to recover a feeling of lightness, then she dropped Christopher Flores at his desk. Finally, she got back to hers.

11
Between special agents, we talk about...

Returning to her office, Samantha was surprised to discover a letter left on her desk. work. She hastened to open the envelope that bore her name, then she unfolded the A4 printed sheet that it contained. She read it:

You are responsible for finding Natacha Stoica. It's me. I disappeared of my own free will. I'm asking you to stop your search. I would be in mortal danger if I resurfaced.

No heading, no signature...

Samantha took the envelope back; other than her handwritten name, it wore no other indication. She went to the analysis lab and slipped the letter into the box. She knew it would be quickly recovered by a technician in a dry suit. She specified by means of the intercom:

"Hello, Samantha Gosvenor, I entrust this letter to you, please send me all retrievable information. It's urgent."

"OK, I'll inform you if there is something. Did you touch it?"

"Yes, unfortunately."

"Too bad, you couldn't know that it would have been better not to. See you later, Constable Gosvenor."

Samantha walked away. Back in her office, she tried to take stock. The hostage herself asked her to stop her research. This confirmed the words of the detective who claimed Natacha Smith felt threatened by her husband and ran away for him to escape.

But did this letter really come from the one she had thought to be the hostage of kidnappers? To verify this, the urgency was to obtain an example of Natacha's writing Stoica-Smith. Impossible to ask her husband. The only solution was to try to find an instance of her writing, in other words, it was necessary to visit the house. Samantha called Mickael Spring who turned up immediately. She explained the situation to him and showed him the photocopy she had made of the message before taking it to the laboratory:

"My name on the envelope was written by hand, it is necessary to verify that this mail actually emanates from Mrs. Smith. What would you do?"

"Just compare it with a text written by Mrs. Smith. Perhaps we could get one from the friend she was supposed to meet the day she disappeared?"

"Ah, but it's a very good idea! Can you get in touch with her?"

"No problem."

"Well, that being resolved, tell me what you think of the message content?"

"I tend to think that Mrs. Smith was afraid of her husband, she had hired the private detective to find out more. He claimed that Smith was threatening her and opposed her decision to divorce. We need to find that detective. Who knows if he did not manage to put Mrs. Smith in a place of safety?"

"If he is an official detective, since we have his photo, we can match it with those of the detectives in our files and obtain his identity. I will put the little trainee in charge of this research."

"Let me explain this mission to her."

"Sure. Okay, you're taking care of Mrs. Smith's friend, and Amina Goma of the detective. I'm off on the trail of Smith's company. Shall we take stock at the end of the day?"

"OK, I hope we will know more."

Mickael Spring left the office. Once alone, Samantha had mixed feelings. It was as if he had taken charge of the investigation... Anyway, she recognized a real competence in him... She murmured: *It's complicated to carry out an investigation with a person who could have been my superior, he is older than me in this place and he is convinced that he would do better than me... Hey, it's up to me to prove to him that I am!* Samantha smiled; she went back to work re-reading the file from the beginning. She needed to put the chronology of events back at the heart of the inquest, it would prevent her from going on the wrong track. This done, she identified the points that remained unresolved:

"The identification of the private detective, entrusted to the trainee, Amina Goma."

"The meeting with the shareholder of Smithandco who had sold the shares after the failure of the take-over bid."

Samantha stopped at that point. It was a priority, she had to make an appointment with this shareholder, but she had to find a pretext. She thought for a moment, then decided the easiest way was to go through the SEC. She reached Denys Dupont:

"I have to see you, but first could you give me the name of the Smithandco shareholder we were talking of the other day?"

"Yes, of course, it's no secret, it's Bert Burger.'

"Burger, it's called like that, it's not a joke?"

"No, that's his name."

"Would you be able to call him about his part in the past stock market transaction?"

"Um, I don't know, we've gone through the exchange of titles and we haven't found any irregularities."

"But you told me that all the buyers were Japanese, isn't that suspicious? You even mentioned that these buyers were known to do business with China."

"Look, if you assure me, you have a serious reason, I can find a reason."

"Thanks! For your trouble, I invite you to dinner tonight."

"Well, how daring! I see the FBI doesn't skimp on expense reports, you're very lucky."

"We find ourselves halfway between our respective offices. If you have a good address, I will trust you."

"OK, let me see, call you later."

"Wait a minute, do you have personal information on the shareholder?"

"What do you mean by that *personal information?*"

"If he is married, what does his wife do, if he has children who have committed reprehensible actions, finally all that could be reproached to him socially."

"Well, you, then! No, I don't know any of that. At the SEC we have no right to conduct privacy investigations, we stick to the stock market unless a loved one whom we are investigating appears to be involved himself in the case."

"Well, it's a shame, see you tonight."

"See you tonight. I will text you the chosen location, I will try not to ruin the FBI."

"I trust you, but know that if the bill was too steep, I would be out of my own pocket, we must respect an upper limit."

"Understood. See you tonight."

After this exchange, Samantha remained a moment without thinking of anything. Where was she before contact Denys Dupont? Ah yes, she was waiting for Amina Goma's answer as to the identity of the detective.

It was two o'clock, she called her on her mobile. Amina answered, a deafening noise was heard around her, a mixture of screams and loud music. Hmm, where was the kid?

"Hello Amina, you have the name of the detective?"

"Yes, it's OK, time to have a coffee and I will be in your office."

"Hurry up, it's urgent."

The young trainee didn't hear Samantha's response. Samantha had restrained herself, she would have gladly retorted something like: *The coffee comes after work! You forget you're involved in a criminal investigation!* But now for some time, FBI agents had been enjoined to be very attentive to their behavior. The hierarchy had not been kind to one of her colleagues who had been accused of moral harassment by a young recruit, even though he said in his defense that pressure was part of his job and that sometimes it turned out necessary to shake up young people because sooner or later they would have to adopt a rhythm of work more sustained than they were accustomed to with their studies. For her part, Samantha clearly preferred to work with adults who had made a career outside the FBI before.

She waited, nervously leafing through the rest of the Smith file. She noted: What about the friend of Natacha Stoica-Smith that Mickael Spring had to consult to know whether the handwriting on the envelope was Mrs. Smith's? Mickael Spring would not be long to answer that. It wasn't so easy to work with him either for good reasons, different from those of the trainee. Samantha smiled. She had less difficulty putting herself in his stead than in that of the trainee. Herself, during her discovery internship at the FBI, she would never have dared to answer her investigating agent she would have a coffee before going to her office at her request... Finally, there was a knock on her door:

"Come in!"

It was young Amina, cheeks flushed from running or shyness or both, if not from a glass of alcohol.

"There, it's done."

Amina walked over and put a cardboard folder in front of Samantha. The latter was surprised that she did not explain herself orally but hastened to open the file. She took out two sheets. The header of the first specified that Loren Astruc had an official license issued by the state of Michigan in 2007. This license allowed him to practice as a *private investigator*. The second sheet featured the detective's enlarged photograph. No doubt was possible, despite the long and profuse hair, it was the same person that she had met, who had wanted to remain anonymous. Samantha whispered: *Loren...I think it's a female name...*She continued to herself: on this photo, it looks more like a woman... When I saw the person, I thought it was a man, but only because I was considering the clothes that this person was wearing, jeans, a leather jacket, a raincoat over the shoulders.

"Thank you, Amina, do you have something to add?"

"No, the search was easy, I went to the licensing office and presented the photography of the man. I claimed I was dating a boy and was looking for a good private detective to find out more about him. I said a friend sent me this photo, but that she had forgotten to give me the name and that I could no longer reach her because she had returned to her family in Ghana. The agent believed me and so, he passed checked the file and within minutes he had the detective's name out to me."

"I congratulate you, that's very good, even if the method used is hardly orthodox and it could be sued in court."

Amina Goma sketched a small smile and her eyes sparkling, she asked:

"What do I do now?"

"Amina, you only owe part-time to the FBI office?"

"Yeah, that's right."

"OK, I give you your afternoon."

Amina would have much preferred to have the whole of the next day, but she dared not say anything and left, greeting Samantha with a sonorous:

"Good day, Agent Gosvenor!"

Well, the trainee's behavior confirmed Samantha's opinion... The expression *little snooty*[9] came to her to describe the young woman. However, she recognized in her a certain talent to act, as shown by the way she had carried out the process with the detective licensing service.

After that, Samantha called the lab.

"Samantha Gosvenor, did you find any DNA traces on the envelope?"

"Yours, that's for sure, and two others that belong to different people. I am going to screen them to see if they are in our data base."

"We need Natacha Smith's DNA. Ah, but I have an idea, if we collect the DNA of her child could you tell if you have his mother's DNA?"

"Yes, not 100% certain, but it would be better than nothing."

"OK, I'll try to find a way to make this collect."

After this call, Samantha wonders how she could get this sample. Samantha joined Christopher Flores:

---

9 Pretentious Petite.

"Hi Chris, I need Smith Junior's DNA. I have to identify the DNA traces left on the envelope of a letter I received. I would like to make sure of its authenticity. If it is Mrs. Natacha Stoica-Smith who sent it, she left her DNA."

"She wrote to you. It's weird."

"She asks me to leave her alone, to stop looking for her. She claims to have found a shelter."

"If so, the ransom demand would come from her."

"Maybe, but that's secondary, we need to know if this letter comes from her or not. Would you have a pretext to collect the baby's DNA?"

"Wouldn't it have been found on the clothes that Rosa Williams was wearing during the aggression? Generally, babies drool."

"There were no DNA traces on her clothes other than her own. I think she didn't have time to take the baby in her arms. Remember her testimony, she went to see him, she noticed that he was asleep, she went back downstairs to prepare his meal. It is at this moment that her attacker appeared. So, could we find the baby's DNA by recovering his diapers in the trash?"

"Hmm, I don't think so. Feces very rarely bear sufficient traces. Saliva is the most reliable medium. Listen, Smith's sister, the baby's aunt, lives in Hinsdale. I will find her, and I will ask her to take the saliva sample from the child. Why would she oppose it? She is aware of the kidnapping of her sister-in-law; she should be willing to participate in anything that might help find her."

"Perfect, I'll let you do so, but it's urgent."

"I'll take care of it today. See you later."

"Thank you, I'm counting on you."

Samantha wondered what pretext Christopher Flores was going to bring up to be able to take the sample, but she trusted him, he was smart and when he had an idea in mind, he made it work...

With the question of the DNA settled, Samantha Gosvenor returned to the trail of the shareholder of Smithandco Investment. She thought she didn't even have his name, so she called Denys Dupont.

He texted her back:

"I'm in a meeting, I'm going out, but I can only devote two or three minutes to you, what is the problem?"

"I would like to have the name of the shareholder who sold all his shares after the failed takeover bid on Smith's company."

"But Samantha, I already gave it to you, his name is Burt Burger. You were even surprised that he had such a name. Do you want me to send you his file with his contact information?"

"No, I can get them here. Excuse me for disturbing you, I'm confused with this investigation that goes in all directions. Thank you and see you soon."

"Soon, it's tonight, remember that we have an appointment for dinner and that you are inviting me."

"I do not forget, but I expect you to tell me the restaurant of your choice."

"I'll take care of it after my meeting, see you later."

"See you tonight!"

12

A CONFIDENT FINANCIER

Samantha sent the shareholder's first and last name to the file service. A few minutes later, she got his coordinates. She discovered that he resided in Chicago. She did not hesitate a minute and called the number. She got the answering machine, but it was Burt Burger who recorded the announcement. She left the following message: *Hello Mr. Burger, Samantha Gosvenor from the Chicago FBI office. Please call me back urgently, I am in charge of the investigation into the disappearance of Mrs. Natasha Smith.*

Even before ending her call, she was surprised to hear the voice of the shareholder:

"Hello Madam, you tell me that you are investigating the disappearance of Madam Smith, I inform you that I have never met Smith's wife and that of Smith I only know his company. I add that I am no longer a shareholder in his company."

"I know; however, I would like to ask you a few questions, it will be quick, do you have time available in the afternoon?"

"Today? Hmm, let me see. 3:30 p.m.?"

"Okay, where?"

"At my office, I'll text you the address. See you soon."

Samantha didn't have time to say anything, but he kept his promise, because a minute later, the address fell on her mobile:

525 N. Michigan Ave. Chicago.

Magnificent Mile, the most beautiful avenue in Chicago, that of international luxury boutiques...

This exceptional address was proof of the shareholder's fortune. She wondered what kind of building the address matched. To find out, she feverishly Googled to see if a photo was available. It was, except it wasn't a building she had under her eyes, but the Intercontinental hotel, a magnificent building. Did that mean that Bert Burger lived at the hotel or that he had set up his office there? She would soon find out.

Samantha looked at her watch, it was two-thirty, she had to get ready. One hour was left before her meeting with the shareholder. She opened the closet in her office, replaced her jeans by a suit, put on tights, took off her trainers to put on pumps. She took the direction of the toilet, looked in the mirror, wiped her face with an anti-shine paper, put some concealer under her eyes, powdered her nose, put red on her cheekbones. She hesitated a moment to untangle her hair, then she decided to keep her ponytail. Contrary to her habit, she did not go down to the parking lot, she opted for a taxi and reached the street. Parking on Michigan Avenue was impossible, as for entrusting your car to the doorman of the palace, it was unthinkable, because it would be difficult for her to be reimbursed for the tip she would be required to give.

She hailed the first taxi she saw. Twenty minutes later, she arrived in front of the hotel.

She was early, but she didn't know the floor or the room number of her correspondent, so she went to the reception desk. After introducing herself, she disclosed that she was expected by Mr. Bert Burger.

The look the receptionist gave her made her uncomfortable. Outraged that he could assume that she came on a date, she pulled out her FBI card, which had an immediate effect. The man turned pale and answered in a flat voice:

"Tenth floor, Mr. Burger occupies half a floor. Take the right elevator and ring the button marked 10th right. I will announce you. The butler will call the elevator and you arrive directly at Mr. Burger's private apartment."

Samantha followed the instructions. Moments later, she was in a hall luxuriously furnished, the floor of which was covered with a carpet of a thickness that she had never seen. The heels of her shoes dug in so much that she almost fell. She caught herself just in time and at this moment, Mr. Burger chose to appear. He smiled:

"So, my dear, you are not used to this kind of carpet? I advise women who come here to take off their shoes. As for my male visitors, they are never bothered. Please follow me, I'll see you in my office."

They passed in front of several closed doors. They had almost reached the end of the wide corridor when a door opened. A superb creature sprang from it, haloed with golden and sparkling hair. She nodded, then stepped aside to let them in.

"Sandra, bring us some coffee and sweets, please... unless... did you have time for lunch?"

"No."

"Well, you'll add an assortment of sandwiches."

A few minutes later, Samantha was sitting in the living room area of a huge office. The hostess came to place a very tempting tray on the coffee table. Samantha felt she was starving. Everything looked delicious, she immediately gave in to her host's offer:

"Please help yourself."

Samantha filled a plate with sandwiches, one with cucumber, one with smoked salmon and another with fish eggs that looked like caviar.

"Thank you, sir, you spoil me."

"It's a pleasure for me, you seem to be very hungry. Enjoy it. We eat certainly better here than at the FBI canteen."

She ate the three sandwiches, drank some guava juice, then asked her first question:

"Mr. Burger, you sold all the Smithandco Investment shares that belonged to you after the failed takeover. Why did you choose this moment?"

"I will answer you, even if I do not see at all the connection between your investigation and the exercise of my shareholder rights. I sold because the stock price had gone up and I thought it was going to go back down. When you have a stock market portfolio, you have to act in the right moment, neither too soon nor too late."

"Your shares were all acquired by Japanese companies. Do you have any links with these companies?"

"Not at all. When you sell on the stock market, you don't know your buyer unless you are selling through a takeover bid."

"Why didn't you sell to the company that was behind the takeover?"

"I hate selling in a hurry. Before the launch of the takeover bid, I had not considered to sell my shares, I had put these securities on hold. Once the takeover bid passed, their value suddenly increased, I then decided to part with it to realize a capital gain, indeed, I had acquired cheaply, several years ago. Dear Madam from the FBI, I would like show you the ropes of my operations on the Stock Exchange. However, I do not understand how the fact that I have sold my shares could be related to Mrs. Smith's kidnapping."

"If we put ourselves in the shoes of the company that launched the takeover bid for Smithandco Investment, after failure of the takeover bid, this company could undertake a methodical operation to buy back the shares from big shareholders like you. A few months later, it finds itself in the majority and its goal is reached. If it fails to work, then it could turn to a riskier solution, like organizing the kidnapping of his wife and demanding a huge ransom to free her."

"It's unthinkable! I know Edward Peter Smith; he wouldn't do that!"

Stunned, Samantha took up what her interlocutor had just said:

"Excuse me, sir, but we misunderstood each other. It's not Mr. Smith whom I suspect, but the unknown head of a competing company who would like to buy Smithandco Investment and who for that would go through the ransom."

"Let's speak clearly. You imply that the owner of this company would belong to the mafia according to you?"

"Yes, or that he would have close ties with the mafia. I know that your titles were acquired by Japanese companies that regularly work with Chinese companies."

"I told you that I could not know the identity of my buyers. I have put my securities on the market, via my bank. It was the computers that took care of the technical operations. Stocks change hands at lightning speed. you should see with the SEC; they are responsible for the regularity of exchanges."

"I am in contact with Denys Dupont that you know, I think."

Opposite her, Bert Burger lost his luster, but he did not pick up the information and only his Adam's apple made a round trip which proved that this news reached him. Yet, he spoke again, while leaving his chair:

"I believe we are done. I have nothing to add to what I just told you. I don't know anything more, I wish you a successful investigation and above all I hope that you will find Mrs. Smith, who would be a collateral victim if your hypothesis turned out to be correct."

Samantha Gosvenor would have liked to find another question, but nothing came to her, so she resolved to accept the closure of their conversation:

"Thank you, sir, for having received me outside any legal procedure."

"Please, Madam, I have only done my duty as a citizen."

Samantha did not comment on this, although a remark like: *You are in the SEC collimator, you had no choice, but you could have told me more...* was on the tip of her tongue. Shaken by a feeling of regret, but not finding the parade, Samantha Gosvenor followed the shareholder who took her to the elevator. She found herself in the immense hall of the palace. Once on the sidewalk of the Magnificent Mile, she was surprised to find that the lights of the shops were already shining. Her phone showed five o'clock, she discovered a message from Denys Dupont. He had arranged to meet her at six o'clock in a German tavern located in an adjacent street which was accessible to her on foot.

Almost converted to a vegetarian diet, now she would not escape the pork... But before that, she had time to go for a walk in Millennium Park, so she went this way.

13
Work and relaxation
come together

At six o'clock, Samantha met Denys Dupont with a pleasure that she had not anticipated. He had chosen a reputable Weinstube located on Adams Street. He was waiting for her in front of the entrance, they descended together the few steps that led to the room where a noisy animation reigned already, despite the early hour. Laughs, popular songs, beer glasses hitting each other and that language, guttural when it was spoken and so beautiful when it was sung.

The head waiter appeared near them. He led them to a quiet corner, isolated by a ramp of green plants. Samantha smiled and after sitting down she asked:

"By what magic did you obtain such a treatment?"

"It's quite simple, I know the owner well. I have frequented the establishment for years. To my knowledge, it's the best in its class. My mother has German roots, I have always spoken this language. This place brings me back to my stays at my great-grandmother's whom I had the chance to know and with whom I spent my summer holidays. She is the one who introduced me to sausages, the real ones, not those pale imitations found in supermarkets, and to beer. She bought it from a craft brewer, I tasted it very young. I confess that at first, I had trouble swallowing a sip, then little by little I learned to like it, so now I would not drink anything else to accompany a good sauerkraut."

"Well, as far as I'm concerned, I'll admit that I don't know anything about German cooking."

"Good, I'll make you discover it, I'm sure you'll love it."

He grabbed the menu and read aloud the list of dishes, adding a comment to each of them. He concluded his presentation with a question:

"So, what is tempting you?"

"I hesitate between sauerkraut and red cabbage, I think I'll let myself be tempted by red cabbage with apples, because I really like baked apples."

"With what kind of sausage?"

"What do you advise me to have?"

"Listen, Samantha, we could call each other on familiar terms, it would be easier and then, the question you just asked me would be a thousand times nicer if it were formulated as follows: *What do you recommend?* We are not in a palace here; we can adopt a simple and direct style. OK?"

"Sure. I don't really like sausages with a thick skin, I prefer those prepared with herbs, are there any here?"

"I don't think so, they have traditional sausages here. I recommend you try the *policemanwurst*."

"Policemanwurst? What a funny name! Well, why not if it is accompanied by red cabbage with apples."

"Well, then, you make unusual associations, we'll see what the cook says. I'm going to choose a good sauerkraut."

"While waiting for these marvels, if we came to our hot file?"

"Let me order first and then we get to work."

Denys Dupont hailed the waiter. Once the order was placed, he resumed his dialogue with Samantha:

"There, we won't be disturbed. How was your meeting with Bert Burger?"

"Good, but I didn't learn much. He contented himself with telling me that he had sold his titles because the price had risen and that before the take-over, he thought he would keep them. Furthermore, he asserted that he did not know his buyers. I pointed out to him that they were Japanese and moreover, Japanese reputed to work regularly with Chinese companies. It seemed to me that when I mentioned this information, he paled, but he said nothing."

"And regarding Natacha Smith, is there anything new?"

"As I told you, I received a letter from her, but we are trying to check that she is indeed its author."

"Could she be behind the ransom demand?"

"Anything is possible, given the state of the relationship between this woman and her husband. I have met the private detective she had recruited to protect herself. Indeed, she suspected her husband of wanting to assassinate her."

"What a story, that does not encourage people to get married!"

"What strikes me as odd about this case is that Mrs. Smith, if she herself has decided to flee and make people believe in her abduction, thereby deprives herself of her child."

"When you know you're in mortal danger, I think you're capable of anything to save your skin."

"Even abandoning one's child?"

"If she is convinced that her husband has decided to have her murdered, she deduces that if she stays, she will die. What is best for a child? A dead mother or a missing mother who might reappear one day when the husband's hatred subsides, or she manages to prove that he was threatening her with death?"

"It's realistic, but it's a drama worthy of Shakespeare."

"Ah here are our dishes, we can think of something else."

There followed a long moment of tasting and laudatory gastronomic comments, even though Samantha thought the red cabbage had a sour taste that she wasn't used to. When it came to dessert, Samantha preferred to pass. Denys, after a little hesitation, did the same. Samantha ended her meal with a lemon and ginger herbal tea, Denys opted for a wild berry liqueur. While waiting for her herbal tea to brew, Samantha returned to the topic that brought them together:

"Considering Burger's reaction when I mentioned the possible relationship between his Japanese buyers and China, I wish you could dig into the question. Could you know more?"

"I am not certain; we checked the regularity of the operations. Everything seemed normal."

"Don't you find it strange that he sold his shares at that moment?"

"No, not at all, the action had just gone up, it makes sense. Burger is an investor, he is not an industrialist, he earns his living by making stock market investments. Don't forget that he has a kind of genius, that's how he became a billionaire."

"Is he one of the super-rich who decided to give 95% of their assets to foundations?"

"No, I understand he refused."

"Does he have children?"

"Not to my knowledge, but given the lifestyle he had and still has, it wouldn't be amazing that he has heirs, here or there, who will wake up after his death."

"I insist, could you take a closer look at the links between the Japanese companies that have bought back his shares and their contacts with China?"

"Yes, I will for your beautiful eyes."

Samantha felt Denys' burning gaze on her cheeks, she smiled at him. The desire displayed in his eyes pleased her, for they met hers. It was the first time in a very long time that far from suffering from a man's desire, she had time to savor his and share it. She dipped her lips in her herbal tea which was now lukewarm and once she had finished it, she suggested:

"Shall we take a trip to the Cloud Gate? I love playing with mirrors."

"Alright, let's go."

Samantha walked to the counter and when she asked for the bill, the cashier told her that the bill was already settled. She frowned and after they left the restaurant, she said to Denys:

"It was agreed that I paid, and I learn that you paid the bill. Denys, it won't go between us if you don't keep your word."

"Samantha, in this restaurant, I feel at home. I couldn't let you pay. In return, you will invite me to dinner at your house and I will come with pleasure."

If it had come from a man other than Denys, Samantha would not have accepted such a direct invitation, but decidedly, tonight, she was ready to let him get away with anything and it's with amusement she replied:

"Denys, what audacity! But it seems that nerve pays. Not only do I accept your proposal, but I will even anticipate it. Why don't you taste a cognac I have at home tonight?"

"I did not ask for so much, but I agree. My car is parked in the neighboring parking lot, shall I take you back?"

"OK. I live in the northern district, very close to Lincoln Park."

"Well, the FBI pays well!"

"The FBI owns accommodations and I live in one of their apartments. You will see, apart from a few personal photos, I haven't really taken possession of the place, especially since I know that in two or three years, I will be transferred."

"What a life! You can't make real friends."

"Hardly, but I manage anyway. What is more complicated is to maintain a relation when we are away from each other. I take advantage of the holidays to see my friends across the country. They also move, I even have a friend in France."

"Oh, and what is he doing?"

"He's a police commissioner and he writes TV series. I met him in Los Angeles, he was there as a screenwriter to meet the producers."

"Are his series broadcasted in the United States?"

"I do not know the rest of the story; I will ask him on occasion. He invited me to come to Vannes, he is now stationed in this Breton town. He claims that it is very pretty and that the Bretons are the friendliest people in the world... after the Corsicans, but he says that because he is Corsican."

Denys felt a tingle of jealousy. Come on, he wasn't going to be jealous so soon afterwards their first meeting and furthermore, jealous of a man who lived on the other side of the planet. Honest with himself, he was forced to admit that this woman attracted him in a strange way which he did not understand. He thought back to that moment that she had invited him to drink cognac at her place and there, he scored a point vis-à-vis this competitor.

The next morning, when Denys Dupont went to his office, he still had sparks in the eyes, after the long and delicious evening spent at Samantha Gosvenor's. He was dying to call her, but he restrained himself. As he understood her, she hated pots of glue, so he would wait, but it would be difficult. To think of something else, he forced himself to look into the question she wanted him to solve. She wanted to know more about the Japanese who had bought shares of Smithandco Investment, more specifically about the links they would have with Chinese companies.

He printed the list of Japanese buyers, it was short. They were only three. He already had seen their names during the investigation that the SEC had conducted into the actions of Smithandco Investment. He went back to the report that had followed the SEC's investigation into suspicions of insider trading and other irregularities... At the time, what information he had gathered had led him to think that there were connections between the Chinese triads and the Japanese Yakusas, in other words that the Chinese and Japanese mafias had much closer ties than the leaders of their respective countries.

The in-depth analysis of the financial situation of Smithandco Investment at the time of the takeover had highlighted its financial fragility. The company had been affected by the 2008 crisis and if it had since redeployed its investment activities, it had remained fragile. Even before the launch of the takeover bid, some of its shareholders belonged at least in part to companies that were under the control of mafias. The problem was that it was only a suspicion, because it was extremely difficult to prove that these companies were really the property of certain mafias, whether Italian, Japanese or even Chinese... The investigation report had noted that the COVID crisis had caused very big losses within the targeted companies and that these companies had been forced to subscribe loans at rates higher than those of the usual banking market.

At the time, Denys Dupont had exchanged with Gaby Dor, his correspondent at the FBI, to know whether a report had targeted one of the companies concerned. He had thus learned that a gigantic investigation was underway after the arrest of several hundred individuals across the world through the interception of messages exchanged by encrypted messaging. The FBI had means of verification that the SEC did not...

14

CHALLENGING THE INITIAL HYPOTHESIS

The evening before, Christopher Flores had received, by email, the report written by the scientists as a result of their work in the Smiths home. He had read it despite the late hour, then he'd sent it to Samantha Gosvenor, offering to talk to her about it if she wanted.

After the usual findings, important information had been established: tiny particles from bamboo fibers were recovered from clothes of Rosa Williams and on the handle of the murder weapon, a long Laguiole. The expert report specified that taking into account the supports on which these particles had been taken, one could assume that the attacker was wearing bamboo gloves. On the other hand, nothing was found on the inside of these gloves, suggesting that the attacker was wearing another pair of gloves which had to be of latex type material.

The next morning, as soon as he arrived at the Hinsdale police station, Christopher Flores opened his computer thinking he would get an answer from Samantha, but she had kept silent. He hesitated a moment, then he called her on her mobile. She was on answering machine. He left a message:

Call me back I would like to discuss with you the experts' report that I sent to you last night.

At eight-thirty, Samantha Gosvenor parked her car in the FBI parking lot. She was floating on a little cloud, the brain still filled with the delicious evening spent in the company of Denys Dupont.

She went to her office smiling. If she discarded her temporary affairs, it was her first relationship since the one she had shared with Christopher Flores. She couldn't hide the pleasure experienced in listening to Denys speak and the enjoyment of his body which went far beyond a purely physical sensation. She had no doubt she was falling in love.

It was in this state of mind that she sat down at her desk and checked her emails.

She was annoyed when she saw Christopher's email, she opened it reluctantly. Well, its content was far from what she had imagined!

She was expecting a proposal for a meeting, it wasn't about that at all, Christopher's email was about the investigation. She clicked on the attachment, the experts' report. Rather than reading it on the screen, she printed it out. She read it twice, then wrote down: *Presence of bamboo fibers, probably present on gloves made of this material. Curious!* Who wore this kind of gloves? Rather environmentalists than contract killers...

Samantha wondered if she hadn't gone on the wrong track. Was Rosa Williams actually assaulted instead of Natacha Smith?

The first conclusion to be drawn was that they had to start the investigation from scratch. If Natacha was not the killer's target, it was Rosa Williams. The starting point remained the testimony of the deliverer of Carrier Pigeon. She summoned him urgently, via his lawyer. She decided to wait for the result of this confrontation before thinking about what to do next.

Nick Kowalski was driving his truck when he received the call from his lawyer. He had left his phone unlocked because of Alan. Sarah could therefore reach him at any time if needed. In fact, she took great pleasure in keeping him informed of everything Alan was doing during his work hours. *Alan drank well, he burped, I put him back to bed, he's sleeping* or more exceptionally, *Alan is crying, I took him in my arms, I rock him to calm him down. Your grandmother taught me to massage his stomach after the meal, so that his meal goes down better. I would have liked to switch to disposable diapers, but she stopped me, she claims that Alan might get pimples from the chemicals contained in the diapers. It bothers me because I have to run machines. However, a neighbor told me of a company that collects dirty nappies and takes care of their maintenance, I will find out, this may be the solution to satisfy everyone and avoid confrontation... I am ready to make efforts because I know that your grandmother is going back to Poland when Alan will be two months old, I no longer have long to stand.*

Nick jumped when he heard his lawyer's voice, he looked to the side of the road to see if he could stop without impeding the following cars. He had to wait. He left the answering machine record the lawyer's words. A few minutes later, he was able to park the large vehicle on the roadside, he cut the engine to listen to the message: *Hello Nick, as soon as you return home, you will find an emergency summons from the FBI agent, Samantha Gosvenor, you are required to present yourself during the day at her desk. Call me as soon as possible.* The lawyer's message had an effect on Nick akin to that of an electric shock.

What did the FBI agent want from him? Why summon him now? He had already answered her questions, he had said everything he knew. He called his old friend who had become his lawyer.

Rupert Isaiah Kantorowicz immediately replied:

"Hello Nick, I imagine that you are worried, but I ask you to keep calm, it's me who will reach the FBI agent as soon as you have indicated to me the time at which you could be at her office. I will accompany you to this appointment. Let's be practical, when do you end today?"

"I started early; I plan to return the truck to the depot around three o'clock. I could be in downtown Chicago about three-quarters of an hour later, more or less, depending on the traffic."

"OK Let's meet at four o'clock in the lobby of the FBI. You will have had time to park your car and me too."

"Very well, thank you very much Rupert, see you later."

Nick, before leaving, looked at the time, his phone marked 12:30. Instead of restarting, he opened the package Sarah had prepared before his morning departure. A long piece of bread topped with several slices of turkey accompanied by tomato, salad, and ketchup. He also had a drink, a large thermos of mint-scented water and, for dessert, an apple cut in pieces.

He sighed, he would have preferred to drink a good beer, but Sarah had refused to provide any alcoholic beverage. He ate quickly, then he felt the need to urinate. He had still not installed the dry toilets praised by one of his colleagues. He descended from truck and relieved himself. He will ask Regis Durand again for the references of these famous toilets. His French colleague couldn't bear to relieve himself on the side of the road and he remembered his arguments: *Well, Nick, do you take yourself for a dog? It is unthinkable that Pigeon Transport trucks do not have toilets. I filed a request with the managers, on this subject, saying that it was unbecoming of them not to equip the trucks and I even wrote to the boss of Pigeon transportation. While waiting for us to win our case, I inquired and installed dry toilets. I found them on a site that sells camping gear.*

Nick left to continue his rounds and at three o'clock sharp, he arrived at the depot. He was on time. On the way back to downtown Chicago, he turned on his GPS and put a recording of one of his favorite jazz pieces.

Samantha Gosvenor received the message from Nick Kowalski's lawyer stating that he and his client would be in her office at four o'clock. Until then, she had time to take stock with Mickael Spring. She ordered sandwiches for both and called him:

"Hi Mickael, you told me that you had an interesting result following your interview with Dorothy Flowers, I just ordered something to eat. Can you come to my office in a quarter of an hour?"

Mickael Spring, if he was surprised, did not show it. So far, he had managed to keep his calm even when he did not agree and there, he could have opposed to Samantha a categorical refusal, because he had planned to meet a friend at the restaurant. He could very well have sent the result of his interview by email. He didn't. He printed the report he had written on his return from his meeting with Dorothy Flowers.

Dorothy Flowers had been adamant: She had asserted that this letter could not come from Natacha. She gave two reasons for this: The first was that it was not her friend's handwriting on the envelope, and the second that Natacha hated using a computer and avoided doing it, whenever she could. So, she always wrote letters manually. She used a pen which was a reproduction of the pen that Agatha Christie was using, an author she had always been a fan of. Apart from the envelope, the mail was printed. I forwarded the letters to the authentication service. I haven't got their opinion yet. I will show you the copy of the letters emanating from Natacha and addressed to her friend.

Here's what Dorothy Flowers told me about her friend:

I have known Natacha for several years. We were students at DePaul University in Chicago. It's there that Natacha had met her future husband. She stopped her studies after two years of college to marry Smith. I continued up to the Doctorate in Business Administration. I am now a teacher at DePaul University. I never liked Edward Smith and I tried to dissuade Natacha from getting married too young, but my friend ignored it, she was dazzled by her fiancé's fortune and all the gifts he was loading on her. Well, he was already at the head of his first company. As in addition, he was an heir... while Nat, like me, was on a scholarship and had gone into debt to pursue higher education... Despite our divergent choices, we continued to see each other regularly. I was aware of Nat's project to divorce. Recently, I had offered to have her recruited by my university to do tutoring for students and thus be able to resume their studies.

The quarter of an hour was almost up, Mickael Spring closed his file, then he went to Samantha Gosvenor's office. The door was open, Samantha invited him to sit on one of the armchairs around the small coffee table. Assorted sandwiches were laid out on a large tray, there was coffee in sealed beer mugs.

Mickael Spring handed his report to Samantha who took the time to read it. Then she raised a question:

"What is your personal impression following this exchange?"

"I think Dorothy Flowers is reliable. I believe her."

"In summary, Dorothy Flowers confirms that this letter is not from her friend, that her friend intended to separate from her husband and that this project was well advanced since she had found a job, right?"

"Yes, besides, I didn't write it down, Flowers told me that she had offered to put her up. She lives alone in a large apartment near the university. It is possible that they are more than just friends."

"Oh, do you think so?"

"I'm sure of it, I think back to the way Dorothy Flowers' eyes shone when she said her friend's name. She also told me that as godmother to Edward Smith junior, Natacha's child, she felt obligated."

"That's all very nice, but if their plan had worked, they wouldn't have deprived Smith of his child."

"On this subject, Natacha Smith had filed a complaint against her husband for verbal abuse, moral harassment and deprivation of liberty, because, she said in her complaint, her husband had prevented her from continuing her studies and working before the birth of their child. Recently, he had stolen her passport. I reached the police station she went to, that's Hinsdale station. I asked them to give me the copy of her complaint. I'm waiting for it."

"Very well. Does Flowers have any idea of what happened to her friend?"

"She thinks Smith had his wife kidnapped by goons who then extorted this letter from her to stop the search."

"Has Natacha Smith communicated with her friend since her disappearance?"

"No."

"Good, thank you. We will wait for the lab result for the authentication of the mail. Are you really sure Dorothy Flowers is reliable?"

"Yes, especially since I think she and Natacha Smith had or still have an affair. In any case, Flowers prefers women, and she does not hide it."

"I understand. We need to know if Smith was aware of his wife's complaint. I'll call Christopher Flores about it."

"You don't want me to?"

"No, we have known each other well and for a long time. Are we finished? How do you find these sandwiches? I took my custom elsewhere, it's really good."

"Yes, it's delicious, thank you for having thought of feeding us."

"Please, it was the least I could do. I think we will have the answer from the lab before tonight. We'll make a point before leaving the office."

Mickael nodded, then he left to join the brewery where he was to meet his friend for lunch, but given the time, it would be for a coffee...

Lawyer Rupert Isaiah Kantorowicz reunited with his client and former high school classmate, Nick Kowalski in the lobby of the FBI office. He took the time to ask him a question before crossing the gate. security and identity checks.

"Nick, if you're hiding something from me, tell me now. I accepted to defend you; I need to know as much as you do."

Nick's cheeks flamed. Yes, there was one thing he hadn't told anyone... He knew why he hadn't spoken about it... He hadn't succeeded... After a long silence, the throat knotted, he ended up recognizing it:

"I'm sorry, yes, I hid information; it's something that I saw and that I do not understand, but I'm sure it can't be linked to Rosa Williams' assault. That's why I kept it to myself."

"Nick, you have to trust me. It will be up to me to evaluate if this information is important or not. I undertake to use it only if it is useful for your defense. I remind you that I am on your side and it's up to me to decide what you can say officially or not. I will respect the professional secrecy to which I am bound. We are going to go through the controls. At the elevators, we will find a discreet corner."

After the controls, they headed for the battery of elevators. There, there was a corner with some seats probably provided for people who arrived early for their appointment.

Rupert I. Kantorowicz invited Nick to sit down. He then put his hand on Nick's arm.

"I'm listening to you."

Nick stared at his lawyer with his yellow-rimmed green eyes. The wall of silence he had built around what he had seen that horrible day collapsed:

"I'm going to tell you exactly what happened and in what order the events happened. When I gave my testimony, the first time at Hinsdale police station, not only did I not remember everything, but I wanted to protect Mrs. Smith. It's over, my memory has returned, I'm determined to tell you everything. That day, when I arrived at the house, Rosa Williams was not alone. Mrs. Smith was there. As soon as she saw me, she introduced herself and immediately asked me not to mention her presence in any way. She added that she would compensate me later for my silence. I was so surprised that I could not answer. She then left. It was then that I became aware of the woman who was lying in the hall of the house. I thought she was dead. Everything got a bit mixed up in my head. Then the baby started crying, it was because of him and not thinking about his mother's request that I did not speak. I was convinced that it was Mrs. Smith who had assaulted this woman and that if I said she was present when I arrived, she would be arrested and then the baby would lose his mother."

"Thank you, Nick, for your trust. This information is essential, we must report it. I will do it. For the FBI agent to understand your silence in your statement at the police station, I'm going to suggest that you had forgotten the presence of this woman, because of the shock experienced when discovering the body and that this memory only came back to you recently."

Nick felt great relief. He foresaw a solution that he had not imagined alone. The last few days, he had suffered from his lie, he had even spoken about it to his confessor who encouraged him to tell the investigators what he knew. The lawyer's proposal took a load off his conscience. Rupert spoke again:

"Before we go upstairs to see the FBI agent, I would like to know if Mrs. Smith paid you a sum of money as she had promised?"

"No, nothing..."

"Well, that's fortunate, because if she had, you could have been accused not only of concealing information, but also of complicity in murder, because it goes without saying that she will be suspected after your testimony."

"That's what I feared, I didn't want to deprive a child of its mother..."

"Don't worry, she will be suspected, but there is a gap between suspecting somebody and proving their guilt. It is not for you to decide. It belongs to the police and the justice to declare who is guilty or innocent. It's okay, let's go."

They went up to the fourth floor. An agent checked the summons and announced their arrival to Samantha Gosvenor. They followed the corridor; the doors were closed except for the last. The FBI agent stood in the doorway. She greeted them, led them in, then made them sit down opposite her.

"This is an official interrogation; I will register your identities. Then we will turn to the questions."

The lawyer agreed:

"Perfect, I'm listening."

After their identification, Samantha Gosvenor summarized the version of the facts reported by Nick Kowalski, during his deposition at Hinsdale Police Station as well as during his first summons to the FBI.

She added, fixing him with a stare that made Nick tremble:

"Mr. Nick Kowalski, do you confirm your statements, or do you have an additional information to provide or a denial to formulate?"

It was Doctor Rupert I. Kantorowicz who replied:

"As Nick Kowalski's representative, I want to tell you what he has just told me. I add that this information had slipped from his mind and that it came back to him very recently. He expressed his intention to turn it over to the police. You know like me that Nick Kowalski, when the body of Rosa Williams was discovered, suffered a shock which caused a violent trauma, which had the effect of shutting off part of his memories. Even before realizing that there was the body of this woman in the hall of the house, my client saw Madame Natacha Stoica-Smith. She was in the entrance of the house, she introduced herself, then she went, without further explanation, leaving my client alone with Rosa Williams. That's when my client became aware that Rosa Williams might be dead. He was seized with dread, he stayed frozen for long minutes before being able to call for help. Then everything happened exactly as he said."

Samantha Gosvenor couldn't believe it. Mrs. Smith, present in the house? Did she really leave before help arrived? She thought of the bamboo gloves again:

"Can you describe to me the clothes that Mrs. Natacha Smith wore?"

"It's difficult, everything happened so quickly ... I think that she had a kind of pantsuit, all in one piece, black or dark in color. Her head was covered, you couldn't see her hair."

"Did she have gloves on?"

"I… I don't know... It's very confused in my head... I just had a glimpse at her, she did not go out of the house, she disappeared inside... Afterwards, I heard a car starting..."

"Do you think she would have gone into the garage and left with her car?'

"Yes, I think so, but it's so cloudy in my head. At the time, I forgot this woman. I only thought about the victim who was losing blood and I called the emergency services."

"Did she speak to you? Did she ask you something?"

Nick felt a strong blush spread to his cheeks, he turned to his lawyer who asserted with a loud voice:

"Absolutely not, she just introduced herself, she probably said something like, *I'm Mrs. Smith,* then she disappeared. In my opinion, this all happened extremely quickly, that's why my client had forgotten this scene. Moreover, it is certainly correct that Mrs. Smith took her car from inside her house since among the images that you transmitted to me, there is no image of her. It is possible that an accomplice was waiting for her with his car. Did you ask Mr. Smith whether his wife's car was in the garage or not?"

"I don't think so, but you're right, I'll do it. It is unfortunate that your client didn't tell me about Mrs. Smith before."

"I told you that this fact slipped out of his mind."

"I rather believe that Mrs. Smith asked him not to mention it, no doubt in consideration for a reward. Know that I will comb your client's bank account. I will also order an immediate search of his home."

Distraught, Nick exclaimed:

"No, please don't, my grandmother is at home, she is very old and in fragile health, her heart could give out!"

"My agents will arrive at your place within half an hour, call your grandma here in front of me, ask her to go on an urgent errand."

Nick took out his phone, his hand shaking. After giving himself time to reflect, he preferred to tell his grandmother that she had to go to his uncle who wanted her. He lived ten minutes' walk away. She looked surprised, but she accepted. Nick then hastened to send word to his uncle, that Samantha Gosvenor reread before he sent it off: *Uncle Sebastian, I'm sending you babcia[10] because the police are going to search my house and I don't want her there.* He also sent a message to Sarah in trying to reassure her: *Agents sent by the FBI are going to search our house as part of the investi-*

---

10 Grandmother in polish.

Samantha concluded the interrogation:

"Well, we're done for today, you will sign your statement. Depending on the result of the search of your house and examination of your bank account, I will call you back or not. Goodbye Mr. Kowalski, goodbye doctor Kantorowicz."

The lawyer greeted her in turn:

"Goodbye Mrs. Gosvenor."

Nick couldn't utter a word. He couldn't wait to get home and help Sarah face the tornado which was going to fall on their small house.

15
Hinsdale Hospital

Samantha Gosvenor was gradually overcome by doubt. Suspicions about Nick Kowalski did not hold water in the face of reality. The methodical search of Nick Kowalski's house, carried out the day before, had turned up nothing. The bank's response was negative, no suspicious sum of money appeared on his account.

If she ruled out the fact that Kowalski had omitted to mention the presence of Natacha Smith during his delivery, she had nothing to reproach him for. However, it was now necessary to deduce all the consequences of this new testimony. The presence of Mrs. Smith when Kowalski arrived attested that she was also there at the time of the attack. However, Rosa Williams claimed the opposite. Samantha had to question her again. She decided to go back to the hospital, but this time she would go alone, without Christopher Flores. She called the doctor who followed Rosa Williams, to make sure she would have access to the patient. She left after he answered her in the affirmative.

There, she went to Rosa Williams' room, where she entered after knocking. She presented herself.

Rosa Williams said she recognized her.

"Hello Madam, I remember you, you came the other day. I answered your questions. I told you everything I remembered."

"Something new came up since we spoke together. The deliverer of Pigeon Transport, Nick Kowalski, said that when he arrived to make his delivery, he had met Mrs. Smith. However, you stated that Mrs. Smith had left before your assault. Can you remember as precisely as possible what happened that day?"

Rosa Williams looked surprised, she remained silent for several minutes, placed her hands around of his face, then she made up her mind:

"I'll try... When I arrived, Mrs. Smith opened the door for me, she told me something like this: Hello Rosa, thank you for coming despite my late call to the agency. Do like the other times. I'm in a hurry, we'll see each other longer on my return. The little one is sleeping, don't wake him up for his meal, wait for him to cry. As far as you are concerned, you will find something to eat in the refrigerator. See you later. I have no memory of the arrival of the delivery man. I remain convinced that I was attacked immediately after the departure of Mrs. Smith."

"Do you think Mrs. Smith could be the perpetrator of your assault?"

Rosa Williams showed every sign of amazement, she opened her mouth, but no sound came out.

Faced with her persistent silence, Samantha Gosvenor insisted:

"I repeat my question: Could Mrs. Smith be your attacker?"

This time, Rosa Williams reacted:

"That would be appalling! Mrs. Smith would have had no reason to attack me. I was coming to take care of her little boy while she was away, and it wasn't the first time."

"Do not look for the reasons of her supposed attack. Think and answer me: Could Mrs. Smith be your attacker?"

"I cannot answer that question. Mrs. Smith was gone, I saw her heading towards the basement door, then I heard the engine of her car."

"The delivery man claims that when he arrived, Mrs. Smith was present and that you, you were lying on the floor, already injured; he added that he saw Mrs. Smith leave from the back of his house, and then heard the engine of a car. It is therefore not impossible that your aggressor is Mrs. Smith."

"I didn't see the delivery man arrive; I don't understand... I'm sure Mrs. Smith was gone..."

"You described your attacker as someone covered from head to toe, with a mask and dark glasses. After your arrival, you spoke with Mrs. Smith, you say she left very quickly. How much time has elapsed, in your estimation, between the verbal exchange between you two and Mrs. Smith leaving?"

"Very little, I told you, Mrs. Smith left very quickly, she was in a hurry. Ah yes, I remember one thing which proves that it is impossible that it is Mrs. Smith who assaulted me. My attacker was taller than me, this is not the case of Madame Smith who is much smaller than me. In addition, he smelled strongly of cannabis. I'm sure that Mrs. Smith does not smoke, there is no such smell in her house. They also have different voices. My attacker had a metallic voice, a man's voice. Mrs. Smith 's voice is a pleasant, clear voice, it has nothing to do with the voice of the one who hurt me."

"Good, but what about the delivery man?"

"I haven't seen him; I've already told you."

"How do you explain then that he, the delivery man, saw Mrs. Smith when he arrived?"

"How do you expect me to know when I had passed out? I can only guess that she might have come back. I screamed, or even shrieked when I received the first stab wound. Maybe she heard me, so she would have come back to see what was happening."

"You're probably right, that's what must have happened. Thank you, a lot. Rest well. If you remember anything, call me, I am leaving my card with you."

"I will, I would like so much that you find this man."

Samantha Gosvenor said goodbye to the patient, visibly exhausted by their exchange, she was pale under her dark skin, and she had closed her big black eyes. She left the room and came back to her car in the courtyard of the hospital. This time, doubt was no longer possible, only one version of what happened was plausible.

If the delivery boy had seen Mrs. Smith and Rosa Williams hadn't, it was because Mrs. Smith had retraced her steps when she heard Rosa Williams' cry. This hypothesis led to another: Mrs. Smith had fled although she knew that Rosa Williams had been injured and her son was left alone in the house... Was the attacker of Rosa Williams still present after the delivery? Could he have disappeared taking Mrs. Smith by force? The delivery man claimed that Mrs. Smith had left through the back of the house, then heard the car engine start. She would have left the house before help arrived. It was plausible. Samantha had to go back to the home of the Smiths, to verify the validity of this scenario. For that, she had to contact Mr. Edward P. Smith. No, maybe it wasn't worth it, the seals had certainly not been lifted. Hinsdale Police therefore continued to have the ability to access the house if necessary for the inquest. Conclusion, she was going to resort to Christopher Flores. She would have preferred to do otherwise, but she saw no other way, except to make a request to the designated magistrate by the judicial authority. However, going through the legal process would delay her investigation, she decided to call Christopher Flores. She did not give him the real reason for her request, she told him simply that she needed to go to the Smiths' house, because she wanted to acquaint herself with the place of the attack. Christopher Flores, after having listened to her, asked her:

"I don't understand what you might find there, the house has been combed through by technicians, but I'm not going to deny you this little pleasure. I will accompany you on the spot, because I remain responsible for maintaining the seals until the magistrate decides otherwise."

"Would you be available quickly?"

"Quickly, you mean right away or at least in time for you to come from Chicago?"

"In a few minutes, I'm already in Hinsdale, I leave the hospital where I saw Rosa Williams."

"Did you see Rosa Williams without telling me?"

"I had no reason to bother you, I had just a specific point to check with her. Unfortunately, her memory is failing. I didn't learn anything new. However, my interview with her obliges me to examine the arrangement of the rooms of the Smith house before envisaging a reconstruction of the facts, from the scene of the assault to the arrival of the delivery man, then the rescue. Have you had a plan of the house drawn up?"

"No, I did not have time. For the record, I remind you that the case was withdrawn from me to be given to you."

"Of course, excuse me. Do you have a surveyor you've worked with before?"

"Yes, but he won't be available at the minute because his office is in Chicago. In fact, when I'm pressed for time, I hire a construction and design company in Hinsdale, they have a very modern equipment with 3D photogrammetry which makes it possible to carry out three-dimensional models."

"After all, why not? Can you requisition it?"

"In what capacity would I do it?"

"You're right, I'm going to do it. Give me his name and phone number."

"Okay, I'll text you this."

Samantha Gosvenor waited a few minutes before the message from Christopher Flores showed up on her mobile telephone. She just thanked him by text, then she called the company. She introduced herself and asked to speak with the manager on an urgent matter. She got to him without difficulty. He was driving, but he was sitting in the back, driven by his chauffeur.

"Hello Mr. Peck, Samantha Gosvenor, FBI agent, I urgently need to be assisted by a surveyor as part of the investigation into the attack which took place in the Smith residence in Hinsdale. I thought you could make a member of your company available to me. Would that be possible?"

"Hello Mrs. Gosvenor, I cannot refuse to respond to a request from the FBI. I'm going to call one of my architects urgently. I'll send him to you on the spot within a quarter of an hour. Would it be, ok?"

"Yes, it is perfect. Thanks."

"My pleasure, goodbye, Madam."

"Goodbye Mr. Peck, have a good day."

With the room measurement issue resolved, Samantha called Christopher Flores back to confirm that she would be waiting for him at the Smiths' home. He complied with her request and arrived in front of the house in Princeton Road, a little before her.

As soon as she was there, he carefully took the seals off, so that he could put them back easily, once their visit was over. Then, Samantha informed him that she would proceed, alone, to a visit to the house and that he himself would wait on the threshold of the house for the arrival of the architect.

If Christopher Flores was annoyed by his ex-girl-friend's request, he didn't show it, and complied with a fairly dry OK. Samantha Gosvenor didn't take offense, she only cared not to have him too close... She crossed the hall which turned out to be a lot wider than she would have thought, then discarding the main rooms, she moved to the back of the house, looking for the stairs she thought led to the garage. She found some and went down, but downstairs, she only found a projection room that was the size of a movie theater. Amazed, but disappointed, she went back up and went to the kitchen, then to the pantry next to it. She noticed a door. She then found herself in the most remote part of the house, she noticed a door and opened it, it opened directly into a huge garage where a single car was stored, a Lamborghini Veneno Roadster in a dark red color. She recognized it, because she had seen a similar one, on the site of the car rental company where she had an appointment with the detective recruited by Mrs. Smith. She couldn't help muttering: *A gangster's car…* She left the garage, returned to the entrance of the house. The architect had just arrived, she thanked him and asked him to measure the dimensions of all the rooms in the house in order to make a very specific plan. The architect remarked:

"It will be all the easier since I have a model of this house, because my company has recently carried out expansion works and we have in particular proceeded to the extension of the garage."

"Fine, but I ask you anyway to take the dimensions, because we do not know if other work has not been carried out since your intervention."

"It would be surprised, we carried out this work less than a year ago. Mr. Smith was in a hurry, he wanted an apartment created upstairs before the birth of his first child. We had to carry out our work at full speed. I do believe that the company has exceeded all its speed records, since everything was completed in three months. In addition, the site turned out to be quite complicated, indeed, the owners continued to live in the house."

"It's amazing, they would have had the means to rent another house, or even to go to a hotel."

"Yes, but you know, these people don't think like everyone else. They have the power given by their immense fortune and impose their decisions on those they pay."

Samantha Gosvenor agreed with this comment, but she didn't admit it. She wanted to remain strictly professional.

"Well, I'll leave it to you, will you be long?"

"Yes, a good two hours. Then I will have to draw up the plans."

"Okay, I'll wait, but you, Christopher, you can leave, I'll call you when this is done."

Christopher Flores wanted to refuse, but after thinking about it, he agreed: "OK, I will come back at your request, see you later."

"Thanks Chris, see you later. If you are free for lunch, I invite you to the pizzeria."

"OK see you."

Once Christopher Flores left, Samantha Gosvenor decided to start the visit of the whole house. The architect took the measurements of the living room, she went to the kitchen and continued her exploration. She took multiple photos that would allow her to find her way around before the re-enactment she was planning. She really needed, at this stage of the investigation, to materialize the places of the aggression,

the movements of the various actors of the assault
and the absconding or abduction of Mrs. Smith.

16
WHERE WE LEARN MORE ABOUT THE MISSING WOMAN...

The visit to the Smiths' house left Samantha Gosvenor dead beat. She had come back exhausted to her office, especially since she had honored her commitment to have lunch with Christopher Flores and that had bugged her. However, she had learned something interesting. She had had the confirmation that her affair with him was now over and she did not risk anything by seeing him except getting bored, because he had become routine-minded and was no longer interested in much outside the NPA. He was more specifically interested in the matches played by the Bulls of Chicago. He had kept harping on about the game of the Bulls against the Los Angeles Lakers...

Back at the office, she had the good surprise to discover, on her fax, the plan of the house as well as a batch of photos taken before and after the work. The architect had done a good job. As soon as she printed the documents, she called him to thank him. He merely answered:

"We can't deny the FBI anything."

Which made Samantha Gosvenor smile, she had once again confirmation of the power of her institution over people. She proceeded to duplicate the plan, spread the copy on her desk and sketched the comings and goings of the participants, given what she knew. She chose to draw them with different colored pencils for each character. Red pencil for Rosa Williams, green pencil for Natacha Stoica-Smith, black pencil for the aggressor, yellow pencil for the delivery guy. She then noted the approximate times of their movements. It is at this moment that she wondered what Mrs. Smith's type of car was. She picked up her folder and wrote down the telephone number of Loren Astruc, the detective recruited by Natacha Stoica-Smith and identified by Amina Goma. He answered her before she even spoke to him, which proved that he had registered her number:

"Hello Mrs. Gosvenor, I was expecting your call, I knew that the FBI had the means to find me, the only question I had was how long it would take. What do you want of me?"

"Hello Sir, my investigation has made progress. We must talk seriously. I would rather you come to my office voluntarily than have to be summoned. I add that it is urgent."

"I can be at your office in an hour, would that be, okay?"

"Yes, perfect, I'm waiting for you."

Samantha Gosvenor literally circled around waiting for Loren Astruc. She decided to inform

Michael Spring, who immediately offered to attend the interview. She asked him to come before the detective's arrival. He came immediately, she told him about the recent information gathered, then she asked him:

"Mickael, you know as much as I do, what questions could we ask him?"

"He told us he knew where his client was. Given what you just told me, I now doubt that it is accurate. I'm sure he did some research himself; he must tell us about it."

"Do you think she's still alive?"

"I do not know. What about the ransom payment?"

"No idea, we'd have to call Smith about it."

"We will see to this problem later. Let's focus on the questions we are to ask him. For a start, where and when did he last see Natacha Smith before she disappeared? How would he have learned that she didn't want to be looked for and that she was hiding by fear of her husband? Has he met Mrs. Smith's friend? For the rest, we will adjust according to of his answers."

"I agree with you."

They remained silent for a moment. Samantha was deep in thought. She jumped when Manuela, the floor agent came to tell her that her visitor had arrived.

"Thank you, Manuela, you can let him in."

She remained seated behind her desk while Loren Astruc sat across from her, next to Michael Spring. Samantha Gosvenor got straight to the point:

"Well, we have to clarify a number of points concerning your client. It is impossible to leave her out of the investigation as you requested. Mr. Smith informed us that he had received a request of ransom from the kidnappers of his wife. This confirms the kidnapping of Natacha Smith."

"What do you know about it? Crooks could very well have exploited the news of the disappearance of this woman to make this request!"

"In this case, they will not be able to prove that they are holding her and therefore Mr. Smith will pay them nothing at all."

"That's right. Well, actually, I have no idea where Mrs. Smith is, but I don't think she was abducted. That's the reason I asked you to leave her alone. For my part, I only took one step, I reached her psychotherapist, who is a friend. It was I who had advised Natacha Stoica to consult him. In fact, I found her very agitated, even confused and I couldn't figure out if what she was telling me corresponded to verifiable facts. I even wondered if it was not her one who attacked Rosa Williams..."

"Ah! You too?"

"When you go over the sequence of events, I have doubts as to the existence of a person who would have assaulted Rosa Williams. I talked about it with Mrs. Smith's psychotherapist, to find out if she was capable of inventing a scenario that would have nothing to do with reality. He told me it was possible. On that occasion, he confided to me that she had been hospitalized several times and especially immediately after childbirth. According to him, it seems that motherhood disrupted her psychic functioning. After giving birth, she was very depressed, her husband had recruited a nanny to take care of the baby. I was able to exchange with this person. She didn't mince words, she told me that Mrs. Smith was dangerous for her child. She added that during the time she cared for the child, he began to cry when he saw his mother."

"How long did this woman stay?"

"Three months."

"The baby is now six months old, so his mother has been looking after him for three months and nothing serious has happened to this child..."

"You don't know. She often had recourse to the agency of nurses. Rosa Williams has come several times, as well as other nurses. I questioned another one who confirmed the words held by the first. She found Mrs. Smith very odd, so eager to leave that she hardly transmitted the instructions to take care of the baby... How did it go with Rosa Williams, the day of her attack?"

"Rosa Williams said she left very soon after she got to the house."

"Personally, I wonder if Mrs. Smith would not be the author of the attack."

"According to the testimony of Rosa Williams, this would not be possible for two reasons: The assailant was taller than her, while Mrs. Smith is short and the assailant had a man's voice."

"In my opinion, Rosa Williams is not a reliable witness. She was seriously injured; she admits herself that she lost consciousness from the first stab wound. Her memory is failing, she can only reconstitute what seems probable to her. Did she, too, make an allusion to the strange behavior of Mrs. Smith towards her child?"

"No, only the fact that she always left very quickly. Did you ask her psychotherapist if he had any idea of what happened to his patient?"

"He is bound by professional secrecy."

"His patient is in life-threatening condition. In this case, professional secrecy is not enforceable."

"I am not in a position to interrogate him, but you have the means."

"You will send me his contact details."

"I can do it right away: Doctor Balthazar Nexter. He's famous, he is the head of a psychiatric clinic for the wealthy in the region. He resorts to ultra-sophisticated techniques."

"Was this where Mrs. Smith was treated after the birth of her child"?

"Yes, and since her discharge, a treatment has been prescribed to her."

"Does she take it?"

"I have no idea, but lately she hasn't been well. I admit that I tended to believe her when she told me that she was persecuted by her husband and that he wanted her dead... But now after what happened, I confess that I have doubts..."

"You know where she is, you knew when we met."

"To tell the truth, I knew without knowing, because I had no proof of it."

"And now?"

"Well, I think she's hospitalized in Dr. Nexter's clinic."

" Since when?"

"Since the day Rosa Williams was attacked, she went straight there, but if it took some time to be sure of it, it's because when she was admitted, she declared a different identity from hers. She produced a passport in the name of Irina Duflot. Subsequently, during her first interview with Doctor Nexter, he recognized her. Despite this, she denied being Natacha Stoica-Smith. Doctor Nexter even wondered if she had a twin... Then he took a blood sample which enabled him to compare the DNA of this woman with the DNA of Mrs. Smith that he possessed since her first internment."

"But then Smith knew she was alive!"

"No, not until his wife's identity was confirmed, and that was only last night."

"It's a crazy story!"

"Indeed, unfortunately. What are you planning to do?"

"Well, we have to investigate further to find out whether Mrs. Smith is the author of the aggression of Rosa Williams, but everything seems to prove it."

"Be careful, the truth is not always the one that comes to light."

"Thank you for coming and for revealing crucial information that will make it possible to make progress with that matter."

"It was my duty to do so and if you had not called me, I would have called you. I was thinking about it since last night."

"We have work ahead of us. See you soon."

Samantha got up and accompanied her visitor to the elevator.

When she returned to her office, Mickael Spring had not moved. She suggested:

"Let us have a debrief. What do you think?"

"We have to check everything, point by point. Where is Natacha Smith's car now? At the clinic? If so, why was she not identified immediately? Was she taking her treatment? If not, could she have assaulted Rosa Williams under the spell of hallucinations? We must resume the investigation from the beginning, starting from the hypothesis of the presence of Natacha Smith during the attack on Rosa Williams."

"But that's what we've already done. What troubles me is the testimony of Rosa Williams who very frankly rejects the idea that it was Mrs. Smith who assaulted her, she argues that the size and the voice of the attacker do not coincide with her profile."

"What did the camera images show?"

"A figure dressed entirely in black, with a hooded face and dark glasses."

Mickael Spring was silent for a moment, then he said in a firm tone:

"If Natacha Smith was still there after the attack, she was there when the attacker came. You must ask the delivery man again. I am convinced that he is hiding something from us... He lied about the presence of Mrs. Smith; I think he is lying when he says he did not encounter the aggressor. If you want, we can interrogate him together, I can ask the questions, he should be unsettled that I am the one questioning him. What do you think?"

"Yes, maybe. Will you call him?"

"No, call him, he'll be surprised that it's me who questions him afterwards."

"Okay, let's do it that way."

Samantha Gosvenor immediately summoned Nick Kowalski. After listening to the message, Nick

Kowalski exclaimed: *This will never end!* He put his telephone in the passenger seat. He was in his truck when he received the call from the FBI, he had parked in a panic on the side of the road. He first contacted his lawyer to inform him of the new summons. Rupert Isaiah Kantorowicz told him he couldn't accompany him because he was in court, he added, once out of the courtroom:

"Nick, you know Mrs. Gosvenor. You have nothing to fear from her, she is a good person who only seeks justice. On the other hand, if you ever omitted to talk about anything, you must report it now. I'm sure this is her last call. Good luck and you can call me back, if necessary, after you have been to the FBI. See you later, Nick."

Somewhat reassured by Rupert's words, Nick called Samantha Gosvenor and told her that he could be at her office around 6 p.m., by that time he would have finished his tour.

He had planned larger than necessary because he wanted to have time to go home to tell Sarah that he would be home late... If he was home... for, despite Rupert's reassuring words, this new summons did not tell him anything good... It meant that the FBI was questioning his last statement. He bit his lip and tears welled up in his eyes that he didn't even wipe away before starting his truck.

He kept thinking, unrolled the facts of this accursed day for the umpteenth time. He hadn't spoken of Mrs. Smith's presence when he first testified, but then he had. Had he omitted something else? Yes, there was this funny... this fleeting vision which he had taken for an effect of his imagination?

He had perceived more than seen, a vague black silhouette that glided like a ghost in the house... a figure who closely followed that of Mrs. Smith... They disappeared... He heard the engine of a car humming, then nothing. He was just gathering his wits, wondering what to do, with this woman lying there in the hall of the Smiths' house.

He decided to speak about the black silhouette... He felt relieved of a weight, and he finished his tour.

On his way home, he kissed Sarah, took his son in his arms for a moment and hugged him. He had the feeling that he wouldn't see him again for many hours... He warned Sarah of his summons to the FBI. She showed apprehension, but she encouraged him to say everything he knew:

"I trust the FBI. You told me rather good things about this agent. She won't do anything against you. I will be thinking of you very much. Let me know if you're held up beyond tonight so I don't wait for you to go to bed. I need to keep strength. Apart from that, I have good news for you, I had a job interview. It's a job I can do from home, it's about answering customer requests and I can be employed part-time. I think that if I am hired, it will be more reassuring for us."

Nick Kowalski was surprised. He tried to dissuade Sarah from working again, he thought it was too early:

"But Alan is still very small, he doesn't sleep through the night, you need to sleep during the day."

"If I am hired, it will be for a half-time. If all goes well, I'll move on full-time in a few weeks, your aunt

Micha agrees to take care of Alan. If I make a living, you can change jobs and stop hurting your back."

After a moment of doubt, Nick ends up approving the steps taken by Sarah:

"It's true, you're right, I'd be more relaxed if you worked too, even if I would have preferred that we talk about it before you make your decision."

Sarah did not answer, she knew very well that, if she has broached the matter to Nick, looking straight in his eyes, he would have flatly refused, claiming that Alan needed her and that she could not be replaced by anyone. She just smiled and put her arms around his neck to kiss him:

"Come on, Nick, go right now, you'll be rid of this chore faster and say everything that you know. Don't be afraid, you should never be afraid of the truth. The FBI will check everything, you have nothing to fear."

Nick nodded, he was too moved to say a few words, he just stammered a barely audible *goodbye*.

He set off for the metro station, not knowing if parking his car would be possible or not and even if he managed to park, he didn't know how long the interrogation would be. It was really more careful and more economical...

17

New testimony
and its consequences

Arrived in the lobby of the FBI, Nick Kowalski tried to calm the beating of his heart. Everything contributed to the panic he felt rising. First, the checks although he wore nothing about him which could pose a problem, but he was no longer in the real world, but in a fantasy world where supernatural creatures had taken over. He constantly saw the body of Rosa Williams in the entrance to the Smiths' house, Mrs. Smith appearing and disappearing after asking him to keep quiet about her presence that day, then the black figure that slipped behind Mrs. Smith's. He hadn't talked about it, but now he knew he had no choice and had to describe exactly everything he had seen. Then it would happen what would happen. He knew he was innocent but what would the FBI agent think?

A policeman took charge of him after the control, he accompanied him to the office of Samantha Gosvenor. Another officer stood beside her. She greeted him and invited him to sit on a chair that faced hers. He was unable to answer her because of his tight throat. She reminded him of his rights, then said his identity. She gave him no respite before asking him the first question:

"Mr. Kowalski, you have told us several things, but we have the feeling, my deputy, Mickael Spring, here present and myself that you have hidden part of the truth. So, this evening, you are going to tell us very exactly what happened the day of the aggression of Rosa Williams, without leaving anything untold, at the risk of being accused of perjury. If now you finally tell the truth, I promise to erase your previous depositions, the one you made at Hinsdale Police Station and the one made right here. We attribute your past behavior to the emotion and upheaval that was yours by discovering Madame Rosa Williams unconscious, while you were living one of the most emotional moments of your life, since you were about to become a father for the first time."

Samantha Gosvenor's lyrics were imbued with a humanity that Nick Kowalski had not hoped for. A feeling of serenity came over him. This woman was trustworthy. For a short moment, he was tempted to confess to her the promise made by Mrs. Smith to pay him money against his silence, but he restrained himself and resolved not to allude to it, especially since he hadn't touched anything. He tried to collect his ideas; he was going to go over each fact in the same order as on the first day of the assault.

"Thank you, Madam. I must say before recounting the facts that on that cursed day that when I gave my first testimony, my memory was failing and if I did not tell everything, it is because I had forgotten part of what had happened following the shock. Since then, my memories have been gradually coming back. So here is what I can say today:

"When I arrived at the Smith residence, I had difficulty finding the entrance to the house, which was hidden behind a thick hedge of shrubs. Then, after spotting the pedestrian pathway, I followed it to the door of the house. My idea was to ring like I'm used to. That's when I realized the door was open and I saw this woman lying on the floor. I was paralyzed, unable to react for several minutes. I thought she was dead. I hesitated, I told myself that I could leave and pretend that I hadn't seen anything, but because of the flashes, I was aware of the presence of cameras. I knew I had been filmed, so I called the emergency services. It was then that Mrs. Smith appeared, she asked me not to mention her presence because she had to leave immediately. She disappeared before I had time to understand what happened. She was followed like a shadow by this man dressed entirely in black that my memory had forgotten. They went out through the back door of the house, then I heard a car engine, then nothing. Help has arrived and you know the rest, I have nothing to add."

"Well, that's more consistent than your previous testimony, and I thank you for that. You mention for the first time the man in black who, according to you, would have followed Mrs. Smith. Can you tell us what his attitude was with her. Was he armed? Did he seem to you threatening?"

"It all happened in a flash. When Mrs. Smith spoke to me, he wasn't there or else he was hiding. I only saw him when she left, I saw him following her. He caught up with her, he walked very close, as if glued to her. It's not impossible that he had a weapon, but I cannot be positive about it. I couldn't see anything of him, he was hooded and wore dark glasses."

"Think, at the time you discovered the presence of this man, could you say where he came from?"

Nick Kowalski tried to put the images he had in memory back in the order of their appearance. He discovered the body. Several minutes passed as he hesitated to call for help, because he was convinced that this woman was dead. Finally, it was when he heard the baby crying that he decided to call 911.

Then Mrs. Smith had appeared, she had said to him:

I know you just called the emergency services. Don't talk about me, I must get out of here. I will compensate you for your silence. Good luck.

She had turned her back on him, it was then that the man had appeared. Nick clarified:

"The man came from the room to the left of the entrance door."

Samantha Gosvenor laid out the plan of the ground floor of the house on her desk, she invited Nick Kowalski to trace the man's route in black pencil. On the plan, there was already a red flattened oval and a green line.

"In red, you have the body of Mrs. Williams, in green Mrs. Smith in the entrance. I ask you to add the attacker in black pencil and yourself in yellow pencil. You have here the four colored pencils, you can offer your version of the facts on another paper which is blank."

"I would prefer."

Nick Kowalski grabbed the red pencil and drew on the blank paper, Rosa Williams' stylized body, then he traced his own silhouette in yellow pencil, on the doorstep, then the steps he remembered doing. He had passed behind the body, he had bent over the victim, then he went came back outside, that's when Mrs. Smith had come in, she was coming from the back door, he was certain of it. He represented her with a green line running from the back door, which had remained open, to him. She walked around the body, she talked to him when he was outside and he had just called rescue. Then she headed for the back door of the house again. Right away afterwards, the man in black had burst out of the door to the left of the entrance and he had followed Mrs. Smith, they had disappeared one after the other.

"Do you think Mrs. Smith saw that man in black then? Did she turn around?"

"I don't think so, she didn't look behind her."

"Do you remember the shoes the man in black was wearing?"

"Not really, it all happened so fast, he jumped out of the next room, he followed Mrs. Smith, and he disappeared behind her, he walked without making any noise, he glided like a ghost."

"Well, Mr. Kowalski, thank you for this new version of the facts which will, I hope, help the investigation move forward. I ask you to check the lines you just made."

Nick Kowalski felt an enormous relief, the interrogation took a reassuring turn, Samantha Gosvenor did not see him as a culprit, but as a key witness to the case. When she had summoned him, he had imagined that the FBI agent was going to throw him in a cell and accuse him of the murder.

He leaned over the plan of the house, passed his index successively over the different lines then he confirmed them:

"I have nothing to change, that's how people moved."

"Please put your signature on this plan, then you will sign your deposition and you'll can go."

Nick Kowalski's face lit up; he was overwhelmed with thanks. Samantha Gosvenor smiled and concluded the interrogation:

"Thank you for telling the truth. We need to find Mrs. Williams' attacker for her of course, but also to find out what has become of her. Your testimony is decisive, it allows us to have a timing of what happened immediately after the attack. A last question. When you arrived, you said it took you some time to find the path to the house. At this moment, did you hear a cry?"

Nick Kowalski recalled once again his getting out of the truck, his perplexity in front of the shrubs which surrounded the residence, the search for a passage... Yes, there had been a cry... Now that the FBI agent was bringing it up, he was sure of it.

"Yes, I heard a cry ... I remember now. At the time, I wondered what it was, but I did not pay attention, because I had my delivery in mind."

"How long did it take you to get to the entrance of the house?"

"Three or four minutes, I went around the hedge of shrubs, I had never seen a similar setup, as most homes in Hinsdale are unfenced and the driveway is visible from the street. Also, the exit for the cars is visible, but there, I could not distinguish anything."

Samantha Gosvenor frowned, that was a very interesting point, she hadn't not asked this question, but it was important to answer it. She got up, took the deposition printed by Nick Kowalski, submitted it to him. He signed it without reading it again. She accompanied him to the elevator. Once Nick left, she spoke to Mickael Spring:

"What do you think? Did he tell the whole truth this time?"

"Yes, I'm sure of it. I observed his gestures, nothing indicated a lie."

"Well, we're making progress, but there's still one question open, which is this: Where did they go, Mrs. Smith and the alleged attacker of Rosa Williams? One fact is certain, there was this engine noise, so they left by car, but where is the garage exit? We must find the answer."

"Isn't that noted on the architect's plan?"

"No, and I'm going to have to go back there."

"I am coming with you, take the plan."

"Okay, but I have to warn Christopher Flores again so that we have access to the house."

She did so immediately, Christopher Flores was very intrigued, he wondered what she sought, but he accepted. They met there an hour later. He raised the question he had almost asked her on the phone:

"What are you looking for that you didn't find yesterday?"

"The car entrance and exit."

Christopher broke the seals. Samantha Gosvenor and Mickael Spring rushed into the house, and to the garage. The beautiful red car was still there. There was definitely an exit. The walls of the closed garage were painted black and formed a sort of casket which showcased the Lamborghini. Samantha Gosvenor examined the floor on which traces left by the experts could be seen. She murmured: *What cretins, they did not push further!* She would give them a telling off, at the first opportunity. There must be a door leading out. She looked for it by passing her hand over a wall and Mickael Spring did the same. A moment later, he shouted: *I have it!* The wall rolled up without a sound and revealed a dark tunnel. Samantha went into it immediately, followed by Mickael Spring, the lights were triggered off as they passed. They walked for several meters, then they came to a slope which led them to another door, quite visible. Samantha opened it, they emerged in street different from Princeton Street. Michael Spring remarked:

"We must have passed through the basement of a house that overlooks this street. In my opinion, it is necessary to ask for the scientific investigation of the passage and this second house. Does it belong to Mr. Smith? Is it inhabited? How come she wasn't mentioned during the first inspection of the premises by the scientific experts?”

“According to their report, they stopped their investigation at the garage, they didn’t try to go out.”

“We must bring them back to complete the search for clues. They should be able to see the tire tracks left by Mrs. Smith’s car.”

“Yes, and what would it be for? We need to find this car and its owner. By the way, what about Mr. Smith’s deposition? We have to summon him; he must make an official statement.”

“You’re right. Now, let’s go back to the house. We will let Flores know what we just found out. Maybe he knows the occupant of the other house?”

“Okay, let us go.”

They turned back, closed the tunnel door, and found themselves in the hall of the Smith’s house where Christopher Flores was waiting for them.

“Christopher, do you know who lives in the house on the other side of the house, which over-looks the street parallel to the Princeton? It’s important to know because the garage communicates with this house by a tunnel dug in the basement.”

“It can only be Hillcrest Avenue. No, I don’t know who lives there, but I’ll find out. If you think that the houses communicate through the garage, it is likely that the owner is also Mr. Smith.”

“Okay, will you let me know? I’ll call the experts; they need to come back to inspect the tunnel and the second house.”

“OK, you ask them to inform me so that I open to them.”

“Yes of course. We’re done, see you later.”

Samantha Gosvenor and Mickael Spring walked away leaving Christopher Flores to take care of putting back the seals.

In the car that brought them back to the center of Chicago, Samantha Gosvenor and Mickael Spring remained silent. It was Samantha who spoke first as they were about ten minutes from their office.

"Now we have this house in our sights, we don't know what it's going to reveal to us. I think we have to be present during the visit of the experts, unless we visit it before them. What do you think?"

Mickael Spring did not answer immediately. He reviewed the pros and cons.

Arguments Against: Did they risk destroying clues? What would they do if they found each other in front of an armed individual? They weren't sure the house was uninhabited.

Arguments for: The house could serve as a deposit for all kinds of traffic.

Unable to decide, he said:

"We can assume that this house belongs to Edward P. Smith since the two houses communicate. Speaking of which, how come the tunnel isn't mentioned on the architect's plan? How long has it existed? Before going to see, we must call the land registry or the town hall, we will have the name of the official owner."

"Yes, you're right, the emergency is there. Will you do it?"

"OK. And then?"

"Then we will act depending on the answer. Who knows if we won't have a surprise?"

"I hate having surprises in an investigation. If it is well conducted, there is none, there are only testable hypotheses."

"I agree with you. If we follow your idea, what hypothesis would you formulate?"

Michael smiled:

"None, before we know who the owner of the annex is."

"I wonder if we could connect Smith's troubles with his business with a juicy traffic. To tell you the truth, I wonder if Smith has not invented this ransom story with the aim of recovering a large sum of money. In fact, we have no proof of the real existence of gangsters who would sequester his wife, it is only him who spoke about it. Did he plan to run away once the bank loan was granted? We must check if he has not recently purchased open tickets to a distant country and if he has an offshore account."

"Given the size of his business, an offshore account is likely, unless he just has a shell company in the state of Delaware."

"Ah yes, you're right, in this state, you can open an anonymous account. I read an article explaining that this was the reason why there were so few Americans in the Panama papers affair[11]. Thinking back to Smith's dealings with China, maybe he has an account in Hong Kong? I will ask Denys Dupont, a guy from the SEC, he may know."

"Oh yes, it's a good idea."

____

11 Accounts opened in Panama with the aim of evading taxation in the country of origin.

With that, they pulled into the FBI parking lot. Coming out of the elevator, Samantha Gosvenor thanked Mickael Spring for his investment in the investigation:

"Thank you, Mike, it's very pleasant to work with you, let me know as soon as you have the name of the owner of the house, we can then discuss the rest."

"OK."

Entering her office, Samantha did not take the time to take off her jacket, noticing that the answering machine flasher was on, she rushed to her phone and clicked on it:

"Hello Samantha, the owner of the house next door is a woman... You would not have guessed, I think... In short, call me."

Well, yes, she guessed, he had said a woman. She could only be Smith's wife or his mistress. She dialed Christopher's number. Without giving him time to speak, she suggested:

"Natacha Smith?"

"Yes! I admit I was surprised, but thinking about it, it all fits together. I guess you want to search the house before summoning the experts. Am I wrong?"

"No, especially now that I know the name of the owner."

"I'll be there with a locksmith in an hour, okay?"

"Yes, even if it's silly to go back and forth again."

"Right, but you could have thought of it before."

"I'll come with Mickael Spring, my colleague from the FBI."

Christopher didn't comment despite wanting to. He would have preferred that Samantha to come alone.

Samantha rushed to her phone, clicked on the Mickael Spring icon, then she typed this message:

Christopher Flores just told me that the owner of the annex house is Mrs. Smith. He gives us an appointment there in an hour. I told him that you would accompany me.

Mickael Spring reacted immediately:

"OK. Meet me in the parking lot in fifteen minutes. For a change, we'll take my car. I have all the necessary equipment for the search in my trunk."

"OK."

Samantha was a little taken aback, Mickael had answered as if he oversaw the investigation. She felt annoyed, then she pushed the idea out of her head and thought for a moment. She remembered walking through the tunnel and out onto Hillcrest Avenue. She had detected no door other than the large garage door which was of the same model as the one leading into the other house.

Access to the garage had certainly been built in the annex house... unless not ... Anyway, she would soon have the answer to this question. She grabbed her jacket, headed for the elevator. Down in the parking lot, she walked to her car to check that she had locked it properly, grabbed the bag of gloves and sterile bags without forgetting her flashlight. No sooner had she lowered the trunk than Mickael appeared at her side:

"My car is right there, it's the shiny black one."

Samantha found herself led into the red leather seat of a superb BMW, which Mickael started smoothly as soon as she had closed the belt. They took the 110 West and then the 290 W. Twenty minutes later they passed the Hinsdale sign. GPS brought them to Hillcrest Avenue, Mickael Spring parked the BMW in front of the house. They were early, but instead of waiting, they decided to cross the garden and reach the door. Unlike the main house, it was not protected by a thick hedge of shrubs. More modest, smaller, it did not attract the gaze of passers-by. They were there with their observations when Christopher Flores, accompanied of the locksmith, joined them.

"Is the black awesome car yours? Well say, don't leave it lying around anywhere, it's the kind of car that is frequently stolen."

"I have a very effective anti-theft system that I tinkered with and installed myself. The thief would be duly immobilized if he took the driver's seat, and the car would not start."

"Oh, I'm interested! Some time, you will give me a little demonstration."

"Certainly not, I don't want to find myself a prisoner and set off an alarm stunning. Alright, here we go, will you open the door for us?"

"Yes, that's what we're here for, let's go, Ruis."

The locksmith pulled out a bunch of keys. After three tries, he found a pass that worked. The door opened smoothly.

"There, do you still need me?"

"In principle, no, I'll put seals if we find anything incriminating and if there's nothing, we'll close by slamming the door".

"OK, see you soon."

"See you soon and thank you for responding present. Send me the invoice at the station."

The locksmith once gone, each of them put on overshoes and plastic gloves. Then they entered the house. Samantha tried to switch on light, but it didn't work, she turned on her big torch. A staircase faced them, there were two closed doors opening into the hall. Mickael Spring opened the right one, it was leading to a small hallway and then to a kitchen. On the table, leftover food, dirty plates in the sink attested to the recent presence of a human being. The oven clock indicated twelve-thirty. It probably stopped when the last person to leave the house turned off the switch-board. Samantha opened the cupboards one by one, they contained few things, just what was needed for one or two people. She came out and joined Mickael Spring in the living room.

A strange smell reigned there. A piano was open. Samantha approached it, someone had played recently. A score was still on the desk, she glanced at it, a mazurka of Chopin... She whispered:

"It's as if the person playing had been interrupted by someone or by something."

The rest of the room had nothing to catch the eye. The decorwas chilling, the black painted walls were entirely bare. On the floor, a shiny red tiled floor seemed out of place. Samantha went to a door at the back of the room, opened it, there was a tiny room with no window. A bookcase ran along a whole wall, she said aloud to Mickael Spring who had joined her:

"It's the kind of wall that can hide a way out, let us try to find it."

Mickael Spring took the time to examine the shelves carefully, then he began to remove a row of books. A fine groove appeared in the wood which suggested an opening there. He followed this line and removed the books all the way up. Then he went across the width to clear the other side of the door. When he found it, he removed all the books to the top.

"Well, shall we see what's behind?"

"OK! There is no visible handle, how does it open? There must be a button control?"

Samantha looked around, but she detected nothing like it. She ran her eye over the rest of the small room. There was a sealed chest in the corner, she pressed the front and a keyboard with numbers appeared.

"You have to enter a code to open the door; it's too complicated and too long to find it, I suggest we break open the door. It should be possible for the three of us."

"Yes, unless it's armored."

"Come on, who takes the job?"

Christopher Flores planted his shoulder resolutely against the door and the other two supported him. They gave a first knock, but the door did not move. He proposed:

"Well, we have to find a tool to try to lift the door or else... We can try to slip a credit card, maybe it will work?"

He took out his wallet and took one of his cards which he immediately slipped into the slot; the door opened.

"Why did they put a code!"

A narrow staircase appeared in front of them. Christopher took the lead of the group; he pointed his phone light at the steps in front of him. Downstairs they found themselves in a huge warehouse. Cardboard boxes and large wooden crates were stored.

"What do we begin with?"

"We can attack a crate, but we'll let the experts continue the job."

Samantha released the tape that closed the box placed two steps from her. She exclaimed, astonished and very excited:

"Have a look at the tin cans!"

Christopher Flores said in a loud voice:

"That reminds me of a case from a few years ago, when I was stationed in Boston. We got our hands on a drug deal, the cocaine was hidden in tin cans. I think we might have some surprises if we open one of the boxes. They may be not solely sardines…"

"I have a Swiss army knife; I can open one without problem."

"Well, go ahead!"

Mickael Spring attacked a box which he took at random, after having plunged his hand to avoid the first layers. At the sight of the small black sardines, he exclaimed, brandishing one:

"Chocolate sardines!"

Samantha suggested:

"Perhaps it is hollow? Cut one in half."

He put the sardine on the wooden lid of a crate and gently split it in two. A white powder spread.

He said:

"I don't think it's sugar."

He crumbled the powder with his fingers:

"We'll have to get it analyzed, but for me it's cocaine."

"Then I wonder why Smith would have needed to organize a request of ransom. Here, there are millions."

Samantha took matters into her own hands:

"I suggest we go back and visit the rest of the house. Christopher, can you place one or two officers to stand guard? I would be surprised if the owners did not turn up to take care of the goods."

"No, sorry, I don't have any agents available, but you at the FBI can handle it. Anyway, this drug must be kept safe in a police warehouse."

"You're right, I call the office to alert the guys of the anti-drug squad."

She went back downstairs and reached her boss, Romuald S. Brown. She told him about their discovery. He undertook to telephone his colleague of the anti-drug group. It was up to them to take over. Then she went upstairs. A lounge area was set up on the landing, lit by a large skylight. She walked to her right and opened the bedroom door. Appalled by the vision of horror that she had in front of her eyes, she exclaimed:

"Oh my god! Come quickly, there is..."

Christopher Flores and Mickael Spring rushed upstairs and in turn saw the body lying on the bed. Her arms hung at her sides; her chest was stained with dried blood.

"Do not enter, it's a crime scene, I'm just taking some pictures and calling the experts."

Samantha photographed the body with the zoom of her camera, then once back on the landing, she looked at the pictures on her screen. She addressed Christopher Flores:

"By the way, what does Natacha Smith look like?"

"Small, blonde, very cute."

"Well, I wonder if she might not be the victim."

"Let me see."

Christopher scrutinized the photo:

"I think it's her or she looks very much like her. We need to summon Edward P. Smith urgently."

"Even though he was claiming that his wife had been abducted, here we find her corpse in a house which communicates with his! It's a crazy story!"

They went back down after having taken a look at the rest of the floor.

In the hall, Samantha took charge of the operations:

"Well, the first thing to do is to notify the medical examiner so that he comes and does the first observations on the victim. We must also wait for the arrival of the scientific experts and the police officers of the DEA[12]".

Christopher Flores intervened:

"For my part, being no longer concerned, I will return to the station. Good luck guys. Hmm… Excuse me, Samantha."

"No big deal, I'm used to it. Thanks for your help, Christopher. Have a nice day."

"Goodbye!"

He went away, leaving them to their work.

The first to introduce himself was the pathologist, Dr. Jenny Mosterring. Fifteen minutes later, she made her first comment aloud:

"This woman was not killed here; her body was transported. She struggled, there's blood under her fingernails, we can definitely get a DNA. At first sight

---

12 Drug Enforcement Administration: Agency responsible for combating drug trafficking.

and considering room temperature, I'd say she must have been dead for about forty-eight hours, but I can be more precise after the autopsy. Well, for the rest, I will have the body transported after the passage of the experts."

"Okay, are you waiting for them?"

"No, I do not have time and I'm done with the first findings. I will leave my assistant, Ernest Hemingson, here present, he will be in charge of bringing the corpse back to me at the lab."

"You'll send me your report very soon, won't you?"

"I will send it to you as soon as possible, I have two others to write before this one."

Samantha Gosvenor was disappointed, but she didn't show it. She was meeting with the coroner for the first time, but she had heard of her. Jenny Mosterring was known for her difficult personality and her great independence. She hated people stepping on her toes, because she considered herself master of her time. To insist would only have opposite effect to that at which Samantha aimed. She had in mind the words of Mickael Spring who had practiced her: *Mosterring only obeys her corpses. She always says that they dictate her conduct, that she owes them the truth, that she is their last defense against miscarriage of justice and that she does everything in her power to bring the information necessary to identify the culprit. The requests of the police and judicial authorities come after those which are, according to her, expressed by the bodies.* It's unpleasant to work with her, but we forgive her all because she is exceptional, she is one of the rare medical examiners to combine the methods of yesteryear and the most up-to-date means, so she has acquired the most recent scanner. It's a woman of exception. His whole existence is centered on her work, on her corpses. She lives alone, does not have children. She gives courses in forensic medicine at the university to contribute to the training medical students. She fascinates them and her course is very popular.

Jenny Mosterring once gone, Samantha Gosvenor got ready to leave the room where the dead was still lying on the bed. Although she had put a mask on her face, the smell emanating of the body penetrated her nostrils. She could never have worked in a legal medical service...

18
Somewhat macho experts . . .

After the arrival of the two scientific experts, Samantha Gosvenor, deciding to observe them during their intervention, posted herself at the entrance to the room where they were going to officiate. Once that they had brought their equipment and put on their suits, Xavier Jones, annoyed, asked her to leave the premises:

"Well, Madam, you must let us work, you will have the report, it is useless to stay here watching what we do, and it bothers us."

Samantha tried to negotiate:

"I am interested in your work, and I must ensure that you do it according to procedure."

Xavier Jones got angry:

"Your presence is absolutely useless. On the contrary, you risk disturbing the crime scene."

"This is not a crime scene, Dr. Mosterring claimed that this woman had been killed somewhere else."

"Still, even if the criminal only brought her into this room, he could have left traces, we must do everything to protect them and recover as many clues as possible."

Samantha wanted to avoid a painful confrontation, she gave in and went downstairs where she found Mickael Spring. She informed him of the attitude of the experts and commented:

"I really wanted to tell them that if they had done their job properly for their first expertise, they would have discovered the tunnel which connected the two houses, and we would have saved time and perhaps we could have saved Natacha Smith."

"Oh, I don't think so. She was killed elsewhere, then brought back here and according to the coroner, she has been dead for at least 48 hours. Anyway, I do not understand why the murderer acted this way. He could have chosen to dispose of the corpse in such a way that Natacha Smith would not have been find and would have been declared missing. We will have to think and find out why the killer did this."

"Natacha Smith couldn't ignore what was in the garage of her house. I don't know what her role in the cocaine trade could be, however, the minimum offense that we can suspect her of is receiving concealed goods."

"I agree with you that she was aware of the nature of the products stored in the garage, but if we consider the testimony of her friend, Florence Flowers, to be reliable, Natacha Smith had no ready cash; but if she had been active in this traffic, she would have had a well-stocked bank account."

"The truth lies with Edward P. Smith."

"While you were on the first floor, I went back to the garage and took one of the tins of sardines. Look, we have the location of the cannery."

As he spoke, Mickael Spring handed her the box. Samantha read the printed inscription:

BRIGANTINE COMPANY
Sardines caught in the Atlantic Canned in Brigantine
Expiry date: 01/01/2025
New Jersey Maritime Cooperative UNITED
STATES

Canned sardines… Samantha Gosvenor's face lit up.

"Wow, what an extraordinary coincidence! I know a French policeman who knows a lot about sardines! He praised the merits of Breton sardines to me. I met him in Los Angeles where he had come to present to a producer his detective series which works very well on television in France. I'm going to call him to ask him if the French have already used this process for transportation and drug trafficking."

"I do not know if I would make that move in your place. If the DEA ever finds out that you talked about this case with a Frenchman, you're going to take a beating. They are going to launch a super operation, keeping secrecy and starting a joint investigation in all countries concerned. Once the drug has been analyzed, they will know the country where the cocaine comes from. The other countries and regions involved, New Jersey for the canning and we here in Chicago, to see how and by whom this drug ended up in Hinsdale. Something escapes me in this business, it is the role of EP Smith. Besides, I wonder where he can be?"

"I think he flew to a country that doesn't have an extradition treaty with the United States. Speaking of which, I need to call his bank to find out if they paid him the amount of the so-called ransom."

Samantha decided to do it immediately. She opened the investigation file, found Smith's statement to Hinsdale Police Station. To back up his claims, Edward P. Smith had given the name of his banker and his personal mobile number.

"Hello, Mr. Fairbanks?"

"Himself, who am I speaking to?"

"Samantha Gosvenor, FBI Agent, Chicago Bureau. Mr. Edward P. Smith reported to us the abduction of his wife, followed by a ransom demand. Did you pay him this sum?"

"Yes, we made the transfer to the account indicated by the kidnappers."

"Where is this account located?"

"Look, I can't give you that information over the phone. It will be available if I receive an official summon to my office."

"Okay, I'll send you a formal summons by email, are you agreeable to this?"

"OK, anyway, it would not do me any good to drag. I just want to know the reason for your request."

"Ms. Smith was found murdered in her home; we suspect her husband."

"Ah! In this case, I understand."

Samantha Gosvenor spoke to Mickael Spring:

"The banker wants me to make an appointment with him at my office, before telling me more about the ransom, I will summon him in the evening. I can't set him a time as long as I don't know at what time the technicians will be finished. Could you ask them?"

"All right."

Mickael Spring went upstairs to ask the technicians.

"An hour and a half for the bedroom, at least two hours for the garage and the tunnel. So minimum, three and a half hours, even four hours."

"Thank you, if you need anything, we're downstairs."

"OK, no problem."

Mickael Spring returned to Samantha, informed her of the technicians' response.

"Well, then we will be free around seven o'clock. I'll put the appointment at eight o'clock."

"I can stay here; you could meet him sooner."

"I prefer you to be at the interview. Together, we will be more efficient."

Mickael smiled, he wondered if he, placed in Samantha's conditions, would have behaved in such an elegant way. Samantha sent the email containing the summons to the banker. She received back his consent.

She still had more than three hours to kill... before she could reach her office...

She reopened her investigation file. Returning to the remarks made by Loren Astruc, she noted in her notebook:

Information from Loren Astruc.

– Same information collected by Mickael Spring from Dorothy Flowers: Refusal of divorce by Smith. Threats to his wife.

– The fact that Mrs. Smith does not want to be searched for: information coming only from Astruc. Mrs. Smith, according to Astruc, was hospitalized at the clinic, but she was found dead, in a house that belonged to her.

Conclusion to be drawn from this information: The most urgent thing was to call Doctor Balthazar Nexter, who followed Natacha Smith at the Carnations Clinic, Bellwood. Samantha Gosvenor called the clinic, she declined her position and got the psychiatrist doctor.

"Hello doctor, I would like to know if you have recently hospitalized Mrs. Natacha Stoica-Smith?"

"Oh, it's been a while, Mrs. Smith was hospitalized in our facility after the birth of her first child more than three months ago."

"Mr. Astruc claims that she was hospitalized very recently."

"He is wrong, she was not. I follow her on a regular basis because she is under treatment, I didn't see fit to hospitalize her. Her relationship with her child has improved a lot."

"Did she tell you about her wish to separate from her husband?"

"I cannot answer you, being subject to professional secrecy."

"Doctor, sorry to bring you bad news, but we have found Mrs. Smith today at her home, she was murdered. That's why I'm entitled to ask you for this information."

"Murdered? But by whom?"

"It's too early to know. When did you last see Mrs. Smith?"

"Wait a minute, I consult my agenda."

Samantha Gosvenor pressed the silence button to address Mickael Spring:

"Mrs. Smith has not been hospitalized at the clinic recently. An arrest warrant must be issued against Loren Astruc, will you take care of it?"

"OK."

She deleted the silent mode; a minute later, Doctor Nexter replied:

"I saw Mrs. Smith on Friday of last week."

"How was she?"

"Pretty good. Since she takes her treatment regularly, she has lived normally."

"Thank you, doctor, I recorded our interview, please come as soon as possible to my office to sign your testimony."

"Sure. I can arrange to come this evening, if you wish."

"Tomorrow morning, at nine o'clock, rather."

"Ah, it will not be easy for me, but given the circumstances, I will manage. See you tomorrow, goodbye, Mrs. Gosvenor."

After ending the call, she spoke aloud:

"Well, we are moving forward... The noose is closing on Loren Astruc... But for what reason would he have killed Natacha Smith, while he was responsible for protecting her?"

"Did you sift through his bio?"

"Not yet, but we'll have to."

Mickael Spring typed his name, Astruc Loren, into his search engine:

"This is what I find: He obtained his private detective license in 2007. He is 50 years old, so, he did something else before, but what? Ah well, he was not born American, he was naturalized in the year 2000. Okay, I'm going to get his naturalization file. The most urgent thing is to arrest him. I sent the arrest warrant request to the boss; I hope he will give us the green light. I think we have to act very quickly, otherwise it will be too late."

"Interesting... We need to know what country he was from, before he came to the US, and became an American citizen."

"We will know as soon as we have communication of his file, I have a friend at the court of Chicago immigration, I'll call him."

Mickael Spring took a few steps away, as if he didn't want Samantha to listen.

"Hi August, Mike speaking. I have an ultra-urgent favor to ask of you. I want to learn the maximum of information about Loren Astruc, he was naturalized American in 2000. Is there an investigation report in his naturalization file?"

"Hi Mike, a morality check is always carried out before the decision of naturalization is made. It is integrated into the file. Astruc Loren, is that right? I'll call you back in a full hour, is that ok?"

"Yes thanks."

He returned to his colleague:

"Astruc, isn't that a French name? Why don't you ask your commissioner in Vannes to look for information?"

"You're right, I call. Hmm, what time is it in France? It is eight o'clock, it's fine, I can call him, I have his mobile number."

"Commissioner Vetoldi? Samantha Gosvenor, how are you?"

"Samantha! What a surprise! I'm Wel,l and you, what has become of you since our meeting in Los Angeles?"

"I'm working at the FBI in Chicago now. These days, I'm deep in a murder that perhaps implicates a French citizen, naturalized American in 2000. Could you conduct research to give me information on him?"

"Why not? I'll put a trainee on it."

"His name is Astruc Loren."

"Loren? This is an uncommon first name which, in France, is rather given to girls."

"Here, it's mixed."

"I see, I try to do it as soon as possible. See you."

"Thank you, Commissaire Vétoldi."

Samantha smiled, despite the time that had passed since their meeting, commissioner Vétoldi had appeared happy that she called him, she could count on him.

Samantha Gosvenor turned to Mickael Spring:

"Commissioner Vétoldi is going to research Astruc's past. Here we are with two tracks to better understand our guy, yours, and mine. Do you know if Dorothy Flowers knows Loren Astruc?"

"I do not know whether they indeed know each other, but they met. Astruc says he asked her about the relationship between Smith and his wife. I can ask him for more details if you think it would be useful."

"Perhaps Natacha Smith's murder will force him to testify anyway."

"I could call her today; I just need to get back to the office as soon as quickly as possible."

"It's a good idea. I think we have to be quick if we want to have a chance of catching Astruc."

"So, I'm going, I wish you good luck. See you soon."

"Call her before you leave, if she's free, she can join you at the office, you'll save time."

"OK, but by the way, how are you going to go back to Chicago if I leave now?"

"Don't worry, I'll take a taxi."

Mickael Spring was happy to leave the house of horror. The priority was to advance the investigation, on the spot, it was difficult.

As for Samantha Gosvenor, she was eager to know commissioner Vétoldi response. In the meantime, she wrote an email to him, recounting the main aspects of the investigation she was conducting, emphasizing the last episode which called into question a cannery located in Brigantine, New Jersey. She attached a picture of a crate and a can of sardines. This would amuse the commissioner who had told her that the best canneries of sardines were those of Quiberon...

19
Samantha Gosvenor, FBI agent, and her Breton contact

After the departure of Mickael Spring, Samantha Gosvenor could no longer keep still. She wanted to make herself some tea, but could she go down to the kitchen? That would make the experts furious, and she had no desire to confront them, especially since she recognized that if she did so, she would jeopardize their work, because they would certainly go through the kitchen to take samples. She decided to call a meal delivery service. She ordered tea in a thermos flask and sandwiches. Her correspondent informed her that it would be delivered twenty minutes later. She was surprised at the short delay. When she asked who prepared the ingredients, she had the pleasant surprise to learn that it was the Corner Bakery. She had her mouthwatering, she was going to enjoy herself. From the living room, she could observe the street, she would see the delivery man arriving. She put aside two dollars for the tip.

She probably had more than half an hour to wait before commissioner Vétoldi would send her information on Loren Astruc. Mickael Spring for his part would communicate to her information on the detective's naturalization file. For a few minutes she left her mind wander on the imaginary past of Astruc. What was he doing in France? She wrote down in her notebook what they knew, as well as the questions that remained unanswered:

Astruc, Loren

Born March 1, 1972, in France. Where?

Changed identity in 1992 before emigrating to the United States. 8 years spent in the United States, before his naturalization in 2000. He obtained his private detective license in 2007.

Samantha heard a scooter stopping in front of the house, she rushed to retrieve the lunchbox. Back in the living room, she made herself comfortable to enjoy her tea. Above her, she perceived the scratching and other noises made by the experts. She opened the bag which contained the assortment of sandwiches, everything looked delicious. She poured tea in the cup included in the thermos flask, hesitated before adding sugar, but finally did, after having squeezed the half lemon. She wet her lips carefully, it was too hot. She seized a mini puff pastry at random, discovered with greed that it revealed an airy choux pastry flavored with cheese. When she had finished her collation, she felt quite fit. The click from her mobile made her rush to her mailbox.

She smiled when she discovered commissioner Vétoldi email, she wasn't expecting it so soon!

"Hi Sam, I started looking for it myself, because after all, I find it interesting personally, part of the case may have a link with the Breton region. Well, here's what I can tell you about Loren Astruc:

Loren Astruc, born March 1, 1972, in Rennes, changed identity in 1992.

At birth, he was declared female, but probably already had an indeterminate sex. Indeed, the first name given to him was a mixed first name, Loren. This first name is rare in France, its choice could also be explained by the fact that his father has the American nationality. His name was Mark Spike. He recognized his child, but several months after the mother. Loren therefore bears the name of his mother. Loren Astruc's mother is called Gwenaëlle Astruc. Aged 76, she lives in Vannes. I can reach her if you think it would be necessary; for my part, I think so. I can summon her to the police station. Give me your opinion, I will respect it, since it is primarily your survey. See you, Dominique.

Samantha Gosvenor smiled; her intuition hadn't fooled her. She remembered her first impression during her meeting with Loren Astruc, she had found an accentuated feminine side to him. She immediately telephoned commissioner Vétoldi:

"Thank you for working so quickly! No, don't move, the mother would immediately tell her son. I don't think he's unrelated to the murder of Natacha Smith. I am currently at the house where we found the body of this woman. As I told you, its garage is full of dope. The DEA's been seized, they'll be coming soon,

I'm not sure I'll keep my part of investigation. They will launch Interpol on the international ramifications of the traffic. For the moment, they need the case not to spread, they will ask me not to publicize the death of Mrs. Smith, involved in the traffic, since the drug stocks are at her house."

Commissioner Vétoldi was disappointed, however, he complied, he understood the position of his correspondent. However, he replied:

"I'm still going to do a little discreet investigation of this person's mother to learn as much as possible. I'll let you know if you want."

"Fine, see you later."

No sooner had she hung up than her phone rang. It was Mikael Spring:

"Hi Sam, I'm at the office, how are you doing? Not mulling too hard?"

"I have just received important information from commissioner Vétoldi, I am sending it to you. On your side, do you have anything?"

"No, nothing yet, I just had time to make the trip. I'll call you as soon as I have had Dorothy Flowers."

"OK, see you."

What could she do now? Samantha Gosvenor felt like a caged lion, she felt prevented from advancing her investigation. She heard an incredible hubbub that came from the garden, she rushed to the window. DEA agents came crashing down to the risk of stirring up the whole neighborhood... She went towards them:

"Hello guys, Samantha Gosvenor, FBI agent. Would you like me to accompany you to garage? This is where we came across drugs."

"Yeah, okay, beautiful."

Samantha bit her lip, the agent's eyes were shining, she wondered if he hadn't been drinking one glass too many, unless he's taken some kind of drug. She led them to the basement. They discovered the boxes and crates. When one of them brandished a can of sardines, he burst out laughing:

"This is the first time I find coke hidden in chocolate! Too bad for the chocolate... Okay, did the experts come by to do the samplings?"

"No, not yet, but they should soon. You can go see where they are, they are upstairs."

"All right, I'm going."

The one who seemed to be the leader of the group of three went up, followed by Samantha. Just at this at that moment, the technicians were coming down from the room:

"Hey guys, everything fine?"

"Yah, yah. We'll take a look in the kitchen. Then head to the garage."

"Couldn't you start with the garage? It would suit us because we have to send the goods for analysis."

"Well, OK, we'll do it like that. Then, we won't be long in the kitchen, we will take the leftover food, the contents of the trash can, we will take pictures, we will check if there are any traces of blood. We'll examine all this in the lab."

The experts went to the garage.

They took batteries of photographs, used the blue light everywhere, then they took the tunnel.

When they came to the library, they had explored the first time they had come, they knew they were done. A few minutes later they operated in the kitchen, while drug officers inspected the garage.

Meanwhile, Samantha had gone up to the bedroom, she saw the coroner's assistant slipping Natacha Smith's body in a sheath, then transport it carefully. Samantha watched him go away.

An hour later, the garage had been emptied. Not only was there nothing left in the kitchen, but the room looked like it had been through a tornado. The doors of the cupboards were ripped out, the refrigerator opened, they had even dismantled the siphon from the sink.

Samantha was now alone in the house. She shivered; the atmosphere was grim. She telephoned Christopher Flores to let him know that the operations were over, and he could come to shut then house. He told her dryly that he was busy, advised her to slam the door. She did not dare tell him that she found herself without a car... She went out into the garden, called a taxi.

One hour later, she arrived at the office. Mr. Fairbanks was already expecting her. Mickael Spring had made him wait. Despite her weariness, she received him in the presence of her colleague.

"Mr. Fairbanks, you confirmed to me over the phone that you had paid the ransom to the Mrs. Smith's kidnapper. Who gave you the bank details?"

"Mr. Smith, of course, he was in contact with them."

"Which establishment is it?"

"It's Yinhang Lai Leung Bank, a small merchant bank in Hong Kong."

"After this operation, the owner of the bank account became the majority shareholder in the Smithandco company?"

"Yes, exactly."

"Don't you find it curious that Mrs. Smith was murdered despite the payment of the ransom?"

"I don't understand, she should have been released."

"Do you know where Mr. Smith is now?"

"Absolutely not. All I know is that he transferred his personal assets to a Lebanese bank."

"He would have gone to Lebanon?"

"Perhaps, but he could also have gone elsewhere."

"Have you ever met Mr. Loren Astruc?"

"No, I don't think so, that name means nothing to me. Who is it?"

"We suspect him of being Mrs. Smith's murderer."

"Ah, yes, I sort of remember something, it seems to me, but I would have to check, he could be a beneficiary of Mr. Smith's business account. Was he, his employee?"

"He's a private detective, we met him, he claimed that Mrs. Smith hired him to protect herself from her husband's actions."

"I don't understand what you're saying. Mr. Smith would never have threatened his wife. He has been extraordinarily patient. I was aware of his wife's health problems. He suffered a lot. He tried to get her treated, I think she was better lately."

"Then why would he have fled to Lebanon?»

"You did tell me that Mrs. Smith was found dead in her house, didn't you? One can imagine that he was afraid of being accused of murder."

"When was the transfer of his personal accounts realized?"

"It's very recent. He sent me the order yesterday morning."

"Everything falls into place. He finds his wife dead. He asks you to empty his accounts before running away. We will check all this. I will ask you to sign your statement."

Mr. Fairbanks affixed his signature. Before leaving, he asked:

"Keep me posted, will you? Over the years, Edward P. Smith had become my friend. I'm sure he had nothing to do with his wife's death. You should look at his wife's associates."

"What do you mean by that?"

"In the past, Mrs. Smith has disappeared several days in a row, which was driving Edward mad with worry."

Information about Natacha Stoica-Smith from various sources came together like a puzzle in Samantha's mind: Recurring health problems, a hospitalization... Drugs in her home... Her unstable behavior described by several nurses who had taken care of her child... She asked the question aloud:

"Do you think Natacha Smith was on drugs?"

Fairbanks did not hesitate for a second:

"Yes, she was for a long time."

"Very well, thank you very much, Mr. Fairbanks. Your testimony is very valuable. I still have a lot to do. Goodbye, sir."

After the banker left, Samantha turned to her colleague:

"Here is a testimony that contradicts my theory! Let's review things one after the other. How was your interview with Dorothy Flowers?"

"Not very well. I showed her the photo of Natacha Smith, dead. She was upset, she immediately accused her husband of killing her. Then I asked her what she thought of Loren Astruc. She told me she thought nothing of him, that she had only met him once when he informed her of her friend's kidnapping. In short, she didn't tell me much, I think she was too shaken by the tragic death of Natacha Smith to say anything sensible."

"Let's go over the information provided by Fairbanks and check it, starting with Smith's presence in Lebanon. He cannot not know what happened to his wife. I think he knows the murderer."

"I agree with you. It will be rather easy to know if he is in Lebanon, on the other hand he will never accept to meet us."

"On the contrary, I think that if what Fairbanks said is correct, he behaved well with his wife. His words corroborate the testimony of the psychiatrist. That's Astruc who told us just what suited him. According to the banker, Astruc was paid by Smith to keep watch over his wife, while he claimed to be paid by Mrs. Smith. Ah, thinking about it... He's tall, he's thin... What if it was him, the man in black seen by the delivery man as well as by Rosa Williams? We have some photos of Astruc, we will show them to Rosa Williams and Nick Kowalski. You just have to use software to dress him in black."

"We can certainly ... But where can he be now?"

"I wish I knew, but, unfortunately, I have no idea. Alright, it's time we take a little rest, I am exhausted, the day was long and difficult."

"You're right, lets' sleep on it, as they say. See you tomorrow, Sam."

"See you tomorrow, Mike."

Samantha put her file in order, then she left her office to go back to her apartment. Arriving home, she listened to a message that had come on her cell phone during her taxi ride. It was her SEC buddy, Denys Dupont. He worried, wanted news of her. She texted him with kisses all over the place, she added: *hectic day, I'll tell you, but there, I have to sleep... Tomorrow will be rough...*

20
Outcome

It was only five o'clock A.M. when Samantha Gosvenor woke up. She jumped from her bed. She had just had a very simple idea. She was going to call Loren Astruc on her cell. This morning, her mind was clearer, there was no way Loren Astruc was the murderer, it was a stupid idea, because put simply, the detective had no motive to kill the woman he was paid to protect. The murder of Natacha Smith related to the dope. According to the banker, Natacha took drugs... She had to check this point with her psychiatrist. She immediately sent him an email asking him the question.

Her brain was racing. She made herself a coffee. She buttered four slices of whole meal bread. She sat down on one of the two chairs in front of her counter and had breakfast. She finished with an orange cut into pieces which she sprinkled with cinnamon.

The noise of the email on her cell phone made her rush to her box. Doctor Nexter answered her:

"Yes, Mrs. Smith took drugs and more and more. I need to see you; I have information to entrust to you."

She answered immediately:

"I can be at the clinic in half an hour."

"I'd rather meet you somewhere else. Would this be possible at your home?"

Samantha Gosvenor was about to comply with the doctor's request when she recalled the instruction given by his boss: *Samantha, you don't do anything without protection. Each of your steps should be known to us.*

She decided to give herself time to think and sent the following reply:

"Impossible, I'm not at home."

"In that case, later, but I don't want any witnesses."

"I'll keep you informed."

The attitude of the psychiatrist was astonishing, even worrying. For what reasons did he want to meet her alone? She looked at her watch, it was six-thirty. She called Mickael Spring who immediately replied:

"Yeah, hi Sam."

Samantha explained to him the evolution of her thinking as well as the strange request of the psychiatrist.

"To me, he knows something, and he's scared... It makes you think he knows the murderer of his patient. She had perhaps told him that she stored drugs at home?"

"Do you think she was part of such an important network? The quantities of coke are impressive."

"The crates didn't arrive in her garage without her agreement or at least without her knowing about it. Listen, if you accept, I'm coming to your house, on the condition that I attend your interview with the psychiatrist without being seen."

"But if he's armed and shoots me, you won't have time to intervene."

"Sam, why would he kill you? He would be prosecuted and arrested immediately. No, I think he knows the murderer, no doubt that Natacha Smith told him about it."

Samantha hesitated, she herself felt in danger.

"Listen, could you come to my house, we will discuss how it is possible to get organized. I'd have to make sure he's not armed."

"I'm coming."

Half an hour later, she opened the door for him. Mickael Spring carefully observed the room. The kitchen occupied the wall opposite the entrance. The counter separated it from the lounge area. It was high and thick. He asked Samantha to hide behind it, which she immediately did, folding her body as much as possible, then he stood in front of the front door. He couldn't see her from there. He walked into the room; she remained invisible:

"Well, I can hide behind the counter. We'll put your cell phone near the entrance."

Mickael pointed to a shelf that served as a storage compartment:

"There for example. Then, I will have mine connected to yours, I will receive the images instantly. He rings, you open the door, he comes in, you offer him coffee. At the slightest suspicious movement, I intervene. How do you like this?"

"I think it should work. I text him saying I'm waiting for him."

"Fine."

Everything went exactly as Mickael had planned. Samantha had proposed to the doctor Nexter to sit on the sofa, she had taken her cell phone and put it on the coffee table. She poured him a cup of coffee and waited for him to decide to speak.

"When Natacha Smith told me about the delivery of the cases of drugs to her home, I immediately warned Edward. He then decided to pay the ransom and leave the country. He knew he could not do anything for his wife. What followed proved him right. Natacha Smith condemned herself when she accepted that her house be used as a storage place for drugs. Knowing about it meant death for her. The sums at stake are considerable. The only thing that escapes me in this story is that Mrs. Smith's body was brought home."

"It was the way to warn members of the network that if they spoke, the same fate would strike them. Doctor Nexter, who knew that Mrs. Smith had told you about this traffic?"

"Nobody."

"Do you record your conversations with your patients?"

"Yes, of course, because I can listen to them again, taking notes."

"Who has access to these recordings?"

"Nobody in principle, after taking my notes, I debrief with the team following the patient concerned, i.e., his main nurse and his aide who are the most present with the patient."

"I take it you erased the recording that contained Mrs. Smith's confession about the drug storage?"

"No, because I hadn't listened to it yet."

"When did this last conversation take place?"

"Exactly a week ago, last Wednesday."

"Where is this recording stored?"

"In my office, in a special locked cupboard."

"We must check immediately that it is still there. Go ahead, I'll join you there."

"OK."

After the departure of Doctor Nexter, Samantha set Mickael Spring free. He confirmed that he had recorded the interview and they agreed to go together to the clinic. On the way, Mickael Spring observed:

"When Nexter talked about the recording, I wondered if during this famous conversation, Natacha Smith had not given the name of the person in charge of the drug network or at least, the name of the person with whom she was in contact."

"I thought about it too, that's why I wanted to rush things."

Half an hour later, Samantha parked her car outside the Carnations clinic in Bellwood. It was eight o'clock. At the reception, they were stopped by an employee who asked them for their identity card and their vaccination pass. Samantha specified that they had an appointment with Doctor Nexter.

The employee replied curtly:

"Mr. Nexter does not receive in the morning; he visits the patients."

"We were together less than an hour ago, he gave us an appointment here. Ask him, he will confirm it to you."

She called the doctor who came to fetch them a few minutes later, he took them to his office.

"I did not have time to check, I just arrived. You see, it's this cabinet."

Samantha Gosvenor followed the direction indicated by the doctor's finger. It was a bookcase rather than a cupboard. He opened it and took out a storage box from which he took out a backup key. He introduced it in his computer and clicked on Interview N° 28. He threw in the key words he thought belonged to the passage concerned with the storage of the drug:

"Garage, basement."

He exclaimed:

"Here it is."

Samantha moved closer so as not to miss a word of Natacha Smith.

"Exactly three days ago, without telling me, a truck delivered the goods to my house. I asked them to evacuate it, but they refused."

"Did you have a relationship with anyone in particular?"

"Yes, I knew who delivered my doses. His name is Robert Strongman. I called immediately afterwards, telling him that the house could not be used as a storage place. During the same day, a team of workers arrived, they fixed the basement to make the communication between the two houses difficult to detect."

"You have to go and tell the police everything you know, they will alert the police immediately, the DEA. They are used to the situation. They will put you in a witness protection program."

"It's impossible, if I do that, I could not see my little boy."

"Would you rather die?"

"Do you think they'll go that far?"

"I'm sure. If they think you can report them, they won't hesitate a minute."

"Yet I have good relations with Robert, we are lovers."

"He is, above all, a member of a gang, before being your lover. He cannot disobey them under penalty of being himself done away with. You have no choice. I advise you to do it very quickly."

We heard the sigh pushed by Natacha Smith, then, nothing more. Doctor Nexter ejected the key, closed it, handed it to Samantha.

"She left suddenly; I did not hear from her. Drug use made her unpredictable. When you informed me of his death, I was not really surprised, I can almost say that I was expecting it. I was unaware of only one piece of data, the date."

Samantha stood up:

"Thank you for everything, doctor. I'll turn the key over to the DEA urgently. It's a real firebrand, the murder is signed. Even if this Robert Strongman is only one piece of the chessboard, they will trace the trail. As for you, forget everything, erase the conversation with Mrs. Smith from your memory."

She immediately left the clinic, accompanied by Mickael Spring. They went to the DEA. After presenting their FBI card, they asked to meet the agent in charge of the investigation in the Hillcrest Avenue. A few minutes later, Robert Seror received them in his office.

Samantha put the USB key on the table:

"On this key, you will find a name which will interest you, that of a man who was close to the victim, and also a member of the gang who delivered the cocaine."

"Wow, what a good surprise! On your side, where do you stand regarding the murderer?"

"No doubt she was killed by a member of this gang. Natacha Stoica-Smith should have known that shooting up on cocaine is not only dangerous for your health, but that it can end badly..."

THE END

Notes

Use of scanner in forensic medicine

This technology provides invaluable assistance to forensic scientists in determining the causes of death, by studying a ballistic trajectory, evaluating the condition of a skeleton after an accident, or identifying, by post CT angiography-mortem. It is also decisive for the identification of bodies after a natural or industrial disaster. The Forensic Institute of Tours University Hospital chose, at the end of 2018, to equip itself with a latest-generation scanner in order to improve the quality of the service provided to justice in matters of autopsy. To do this, he turned to Fujifilm and acquired its new FCT Speedia 64-bar scanner. It thus became the first French forensic institute to be equipped with a Fujifilm scanner.

"This modality is unanimous, in particular for Professor Pauline Saint-Martin, head of the forensic institute of Tours: The institute receives around 2,500 victims per year, for 250 autopsies, always in the context of legal proceedings. The acquisition of our

FCT Speedia scanner will improve the quality of the work we do for the investigation services, the purpose of which is in particular to find the causes of death, in the interest of the victims and their loved ones.", she said.

TABLE OF CONTENTS

AUTHOR'S ACKNOWLEDGMENTS

A big thank you to all of you, my readers who allow me to continue the adventure of writing! Do not hesitate to write to me, to give me your opinion. If you leave your email address, you could have a nice surprise!

If you are used to commissioner Vétoldi, don't despair, he will come back in the next novel. Just give me time to write it, but maybe in the meantime you will be seduced by Samantha Gosvenor? She should continue her career as an FBI agent...

I am grateful to everyone who helped improve this novel.

Among them, the many deliverers I met, my proofreaders, Marie Berchoud, Mireille Schmitt, Françoise Herr-Shrameck, and especially Olivier Auberger and Danièle Godard who translated this novel.

I do not forget those who encouraged me, from my beginnings as an author, Alain Boulonne, then director of *L'Yonne Républicaine*, which offered me my first publication in the form of two serials published during the summer of 2003, then the summer of 2004. *Attentat à Belle-Île* and *Le Ruban rouge*, then became published novels; Eric de Saint Perier, former Secretary General of the Prix du Quai des Orfèvres who selected my novels several times.

Thanks to the Internet platforms that allow me to broadcast news of my novels,

Facebook
www.facebook.com/petitspolarsentreamis/
and Linkedin
www.linkedin.com/in/susan-degeninville-4552a211a/

I do not forget the Internet bookstores:
www.amazon.fr/s?k=susan+degeninville
and www.amazon.com

www.journaux.fr/recherche.php?txtRecherche=-susan+degeninville
which give me the possibility of publishing.

Goodbye,
Susan Degeninville
https://sdegeninville.com
https://petitspolarsentreamis.blogspot.com